G5, Gee Whiz

by

L. J. Martin

This one's for my brother
Rex L. Martin
who's aviation expertise is over the top,
who graduated from Navy Flight School
with the highest grades ever received,
and who went on to fly Crusaders (F8U's)
off the *Ranger*!

Special thanks to editor extraordinaire **Ann LaFarge** and her incisive pencil.

Create Space Edition
Copyright 2014 L. J. Martin

Wolfpack Publishing
48 Rock Creek Road
Clinton, Montana 59825

ISBN: 978-1-62918-190-5

All rights reserved. No part of this book may be reproduced by any means without the prior written consent of the publisher, other than brief quotes for reviews.

Chapter One

After you've sent a dozen men to hell—where they damn well belonged—a little respite is in order. Respite, and a good woman to soothe your wounds.

Peace, at last, by the pool in Vegas, with a beautiful lady by my side...but peace has never been on top of my priority list, and it doesn't take long until the urge to kick-ass kicks into gear. It seems to be an inverse reaction in my psyche—when my pain decreases and my wounds heal, my aggression and craving for adrenaline increases.

I know, I know, it's a personality flaw, or so the women in my life have oft told me—usually with great disdain, but occasionally, thank God, with increased interest.

Prather K. Wedgeworth, or I should say one of his secretaries, called at least sixteen times during the two weeks it took me to heal up from my last repairman job in Williston, North Dakota where I was helping out—for a substantial fee—my old CO from my Marine Recon unit in Iraq. The dope trade was costing his company at least a mil a year in accidents, insurance premium increases, and down time so I flushed some of the scum down the drain. But it cost me a concussion from a 150 grain across my battle helmet, a deep crease across my back, one gouge across a thigh, and a punch in and out of my side that clipped a rib but thank God not a bowel...all from AK47's badly aimed, I'm thrilled and lucky to recall. I'm still not 100%, but right enough to deal with some dot com billionaire in Santa Barbara, or more precisely Montecito, and to help recover his fifty mil G5 that's gone missing.

I hope against all hope that he's not an arrogant prick who's impossible to deal with, as I refuse to kowtow, even for a seven-figure fee. But I'm sure East Valley Road, which is lined with ten million buck and up estates, enjoys the presence of more pricks than the average thirty foot tall Saguaro cactus.

You see, a Grumman G5 is the ultimate in private business aircraft. Properly appointed, it costs a cool fifty million. This guy, who's so smart in the world of hyperspace, was a dummy and didn't have it insured, as there was no lien holder who insisted upon same, as Mr. Wedgeworth paid cash. He offered a cool half million right off the bat, which means he'll pay me what the recovery is worth, and that's a minimum of five percent, or two and a half million.

After all, those of us who dabble in the recovery biz often command fees up to twenty percent, even higher if the danger coefficient is super high.

I have four vehicles, but don't think it's appropriate to arrive in my van, my F150, or on my Harley Sportster, so I'm driving what I imagine would be considered chic in Montecito, my 1957 tricked out red and white Corvette. After all Lamborghinis, Maseratis, Jags, and Porsches are blasé in and around this posh area of the California coast. Leaving Vegas before dawn, I've enjoyed a leisurely drive over, hearing everything Willy and Whalen have to offer on Sirius and then getting deep into Katy Perry...that's wishful thanking and a Freudian slip.

It's one of those glorious February days that make half the world want to migrate to California—temp in the seventies with the hint of a sea breeze, clear, with the offshore islands looking so close you could swim there. It's nice enough that I stop in Santa Clarita and put the top down on the Vette. As my military cut couldn't be messed up with anything but a razor, I have no worries there, except for the fact I still have a couple of angry scars from splits on my noggin from baseball bats or pipes that a half dozen guys used on me behind a joint called Big Rosie's up in Williston. Both cuts took a dozen stitches to close, and don't add to my boyish good looks. But I yam who I yam, as my fellow Navy type, Popeye, would say...even though I hate to quote a squib.

And I'm as properly attired as I get, in blue blazer with cute brass buttons, powder blue button down shirt, khaki slacks, and brown belt to match my loafers. I'd have gone sockless and worn an ascot—as if I had one—but I'd be afraid one of the local trust fund darlings would pass out from heart palpitations or one of the guys would try to give me a hug upon introduction.

I don't mind a good chest bump, and hoora, if it's a fellow Marine Recon jarhead I served with in Desert Storm, but I draw the line at that.

Two Mexican gardeners are working the beds along the one hundred foot drive up to the gate to the Wedgeworth estate. I give them a wave as I pass, and smile when they look surprised. I guess they're used to being invisible to the local gentry.

The fifteen foot tall wrought iron gates blocking my passage—looking like an entrance to a medieval city, not a residence—are set in an elaborate stone arch flanked by eight foot stone walls, are tipped with gold on top, and the stone guard house probably cost more than the house where my parents raised me in Sheridan, Wyoming, God rest their souls.

Idling to a stop near an open window facing the driveway, it's all I can do not to smile. I can see a quarter mile beyond the gates through the live oaks and eucalyptus, and still cannot see the house.

The guy behind the guard window, who has a half dozen monitors in front of him, doesn't wait, but exits and walks directly to my door. "Mr. Reardon?" he inquires.

And I thought I was nicely dressed! This guy is in a black suit, white shirt and black tie, and the only way you might think he was one of the help is that he looks as if he came straight from Gold's Gym before he dressed for work, after he'd done a few reps with about four hundred pounds...plus he has on a black bill cap with a big gold, WEDGEWORTH embroidered across the front.

"I've got an appointment," I answer.

"May I see a picture ID?" he asks, with steel blue eyes drilling me.

I'm less than a little surprised to get a glance at something blued hanging under his left arm in a tidy shoulder holster. It's no bigger, I'm happy to note, than the one in the middle of my back. My swinging dick is as big as his.

I produce one of my half dozen driver's licenses, making sure before I hand it over that it's the only legit one of the six and has not only my picture, but Mike Reardon in the text. He studies it carefully, flashes another long glance at me, then back at the license, back at me, and hands it back.

"You'll have to make this turn around—" for a second I think I'm being dismissed, then he adds—"and go back about a half mile to another gated entrance on the ocean side of the road, that's Birnam Wood Country Club. Mr.

Wedgeworth is inside and they'll call him out when you arrive, if you'll step into the pro shop and ask. Your meeting is rescheduled for the bar there, or more likely on one of the benches overlooking the course."

I smile, give the well dressed and very polite no-neck guard a nod, and as directed take a turn around the guard house and head back out.

Even though it appears I'm not being allowed to see the residence—castle is a better word—and am being relegated to a bench overlooking the golf course to talk about a seven figure deal, it's too beautiful a day, and much too pretty a drive back down East Valley Road with its overhanging oaks and eucalypti, to get my panties in a twist.

This guardhouse is equally nice, but the guard here smiles and nods and looks as if he rides his bike to work—I mean Schwinn not Harley—and could, maybe, press eighty pounds on his best day. I give him my name and, without checking my license, he gives me directions to the clubhouse, which I follow.

There's a guy under a porte-cochere who's parking cars—if the valet parking sign next to him means anything—in front of a ten thousand square foot, or larger, club house, although there are no cars awaiting parking. I choose to park myself and do so, and walk to a smaller structure sixty feet to the south of the main building, which, being clever, I deduce is the Pro Shop. I guess the putting green at its side was my first clue.

Two guys are working inside, all flashy Colgate smiles as big as those of the little alligators on their shirts, and one of them calls the main building promptly when I introduce myself. Then the younger one escorts me to a bench at the far side of a putting green that looks as if it might have been manicured by a guy with barber's scissors.

As I'm overlooking an equally beautiful golf course, each fairway flanked by a multitude of multi-million dollar homes, I'm trying to remember what I've read about the place. Had I known our meeting was to take place here, I'd have Googled it, but I have worked out of Santa Barbara quite a bit, and remember reading that Birnam Wood is considered as elite as any East Coast Club, and maybe more so.

There's absolutely no one playing the course, which is not unusual for these very high-end clubs.

I can see up to the main building, and observe a tall and surprisingly young man, who looks like Wedgeworth's pictures, exit and stride meaningfully down the walk coming the way of the Pro Shop. And as I'm looking back, I see another guy, this one with military bearing, in windbreaker, jeans, and hiking boots, trotting across the parking lot. Although he's tidily dressed, my hackles rise on the back of my neck and I'm instinctively on my feet, moving their way.

The young guy looks up in surprise, and surprise turns to wide-eyed fear as the trotter stops in front of him and sticks a corncob-sized finger in his chest. I'm still too far away to hear what's being said, but it's being said with a loud voice, and the young guy's eyes are flared round as saucers. He's wearing a very expensive looking sweater, and just as I near, the big boy gathers it in a wad in one hand and backhands the younger one with the other.

Before he can bring the forehand back, I'm on him. Grabbing the offending hand with both hands, I use a simple Judo takedown, cranking the hand up and inside and putting him on his knees. His surprised look tells me he's not used to being under someone's control.

I'm still a long way from being back to full function physically, but I took him from behind and by surprise. I keep the wristlock on him as the young guy, who I presume is Wedgeworth, sinks to his knees, obviously dazed by the slap.

As I have no idea what's going down, or who the players are, I give the big ol' boy on his knees a hard look, press the twist a little tighter, and ask, "Aren't you working way under your weight class here?"

He doesn't answer, but tries to come back against the twist, so I take him to his back, but underestimate him as he manages to spin, hook a toe behind my heel, and kick me a solid one to the knee with the free foot. I go over backward into the azaleas...not hurt, but embarrassed.

We're both clamoring to our feet, but he beats me, as I'm tangled in the greenery. Instead of coming after me, he uses the same hiking boot to kick the young guy in the chest, and he does an end'o into the flower beds.

What I presume is some kind of business argument or domestic spat suddenly turns deadly, as I realize he's spun back to me and is going to the small of his back under his windbreaker. We both come up with our semi-automatics at the same instant. We're only ten feet apart and I left my Kevlar home...who'd a thunk it in a place like this?

There's no missing at this range.

Chapter Two

"Wait...wait," the young guy, now sitting on his butt on the ground, manages to spit out, even though his eyes are spinning and he's choking from the kick. "Wait...wait...I'll pay up."

Neither of us is cutting our eyes away from the other, or blinking, and both are staring across the sights of our automatics. I can see by his stance—side to me, one hand resting carefully on the butt of the automatic I'm looking down the barrel of—that this is not his first rodeo. And I'm counting on it; an amateur might have already fired. This guy is too cool.

"I'm going to back away," he says, his voice low and raspy. I've finally gotten a good look at him—square jawed, blue eyes like lasers, black hair tight to his scalp like a military cut, a scar on his left cheekbone like someone got in a good right cross sometime in the past and split it about eight stitches worth. He's got an afternoon beard, but is nicely groomed.

"You do that," I reply.

"I'll pay up, Henry," the kid says, with a spit and cough.

"You fuckin' well better," the guy he called Henry says as he's backing away. He gets fifty feet into the parking lot before he spins on his heel, and hauls ass, and disappears into the shrubs, forty yards away.

I reach down and offer my hand to the kid, and pull him to his feet.

"Golly," he says, a little out of breath, "that almost got out of hand."

"I'd say it did get out of hand," and I extend mine. "I'm Mike Reardon."

"I was hoping you were my appointment."

"If you're Prather K. Wedgeworth, I am."

"You better put that away," he says, glancing at the Glock still hanging in hand at my side, and I turn to see him watching a Santa Barbara County Sheriff's car pull into the lot.

"They didn't waste any time," I offer.

"We get very good service here in Montecito...I think he may have bruised my ribs."

"No question you get good service," I say, as the gray haired fellow from the pro shop strides out to meet the sheriff. He points to where 'Henry' disappeared into the brush, and the sheriff guns it across the lot and jumps out and fades into the shrubbery.

The guy I presume is the pro walks to us. "You okay, Mr. Wedgeworth?"

"I'm fine, Freddy, bruised a little maybe," he says, then back to me. "I don't often have a cocktail until after five, but I think I could use one. Let's go inside."

As I follow I decide I've passed muster at least enough to be allowed into the bar. And I'm impressed, as it's all dark woods, leather seats, and great paintings of the world's best golf courses in frames that cost a month's salary for the average guy. Who knows what the paintings are worth.

He, of course, orders a twenty five year old single-malt Scotch, neat, and I stick with the Jack Daniels and water.

There's no one else in the bar, but I can hear some conversations from down the hall, which I presume is the club restaurant.

While the bartender is making our drinks, Wedgeworth sighs deeply, then asks, as he stares at me, unblinking and still wide-eyed, "I presume that's something you've done before?"

"Pull my weapon?" I ask and he nods. "A couple of times. You can't be in my business and not."

"Gee whiz, I'm not sure I could ever get used to that...I'm still shaking, and he was aiming at you...of course he was mad at me."

I shrug. "It's over now." I'm smiling to myself. Let's see, it's golly and gee whiz from this guy, and he's a multi billionaire. And I figured he'd be a kick-ass-and-take-names type.

"You're not interested in what that was all about?" he asks as the bartender delivers our drinks.

"Sure, it's always nice to know why a guy is waving an automatic in your face."

He takes a long draw on the scotch, then offers, "He was head of my security team. I had to have my vice president let him go and he thinks he has a bonus coming. He doesn't, as the G5 was filched right out from under his people."

"And the bonus was conditional upon...?"

"Well, technically, upon him staying two years...which he did, but right after that, twenty six months to be exact, the plane was stolen."

I smile tightly. "But he stayed two years?"

"Yes," he replies, and gives me as hard a glare as his rather baby face looks can muster. "Have you ever lost a fifty million dollar aircraft...or anything else worth that kind of money?"

"Hardly. That's between you and...Henry, you called him?"

"Henry Hausman."

"Hausman, spelled how?"

He takes another sip and eyes me again. "You don't need to worry about him. He won't bother you again."

"Just like to know whose gun barrel I'm staring down."

"Let's get onto the business at hand. I have a golf game at two."

"Sure. You want your plane back."

"I'll pay a half million for its recovery—"

"Sorry, but it's a fifty million dollar airplane, and I don't work that cheap."

"You consider a half million cheap?"

"Mr. Wedgeworth, when someone has something worth fifty million, they generally want to hang onto it, and will do just about anything to do so. These are likely very determined and very capable people who are now in possession of your airplane...and they won't give it up easily. I may end up paying a half million in bribes or *mordida*—"

"What's that?"

"*Mordida*, that's how most of South America operates. It's a bribe, as well."

"So, you think the plane is in South America?"

"I have no idea where it might be, but it's in the hands of someone willing to steal it, and probably more than willing to kill to keep it...particularly if they're in a country where the law is on their side, which is likely the case by now."

"So, how much?"

"Three million. Three hundred thousand up front, nothing more if we fail."

He laughs and shakes his head. "That's out of the question."

I rise. "Then thanks for the drink...unless I owe, of course."

"I can handle the drink."

I nod, and head out the way I came in. Just as I reach the door, he calls after me, "Mr. Reardon."

I stop and turn. "Drop over to the house about seven, after my game. We'll have another cocktail and talk some more. I'll have a counter offer for you."

I nod, shrug, wave over my shoulder, and am gone. A counter offer is good.

As soon as I wheel back out onto East Valley Road, I voice activate my iPhone and call Pax to see what he can dig up on Henry Housman, then call an old friend, Detective Horace Alderman, Santa Barbara Police Department. To my surprise he's in the office.

"Alderman," he answers.

"Free lunch, Ho-man," I say.

"A voice from the friggin' past," he says with a chuckle. "I figured you'd be looking up at lily roots by now."

"You know mere mortals will never touch this hide of mine."

He laughs. "As I recall, you got enough scars to belie that bit of wishful thinking."

"You got me there. In fact I've got a few news ones since we last broke bread. I'm buying...Café del Sol?"

"And I'm trying to get shed of this gut...but how can I refuse a free lunch?"

"A half-hour?"

"It's a patio day."

I'm closer to the Mexican restaurant across from Santa Barbara's bird refuge than Ho-man is, so I'm waiting on the patio when he arrives. I haven't see him in over a year, but he hasn't changed much—a flat top cut right out of the fifties, but gone gray, a frumpy wrinkled sport coat, and a shirt that's straining at the buttons from forgetting to push away from the table. I rise and shake with him before he takes a seat across from me.

He eyes me suspiciously. "Okay, Mike me lad, what the hell kind of trouble are you bringing to my pretty little town?"

"Trying to land a gig on the Wedgeworth airplane heist."

"You having to chase biz now?"

"Actually, Wedgeworth's been chasing me."

"As you know, I work homicide and that was a grand theft bit so it wasn't my case."

I laugh. "I didn't invite you to lunch to talk business. I figured I owe you one...however, there is one thing."

"As if I didn't fucking well know."

"Actually I just thought of it. I do have some unfinished business here in your pretty little town."

"So you are buying?"

"I am...I was anyway."

The girl arrives and we order, both of us sticking to iced tea as he's on duty and I have a meeting yet today, and maybe I can save the deal I came to make.

The girl leaves, and I remind him of a gig I had wherein my client got her head removed by some cartel boys, and one of them, at least a name that came up, still roams the streets of Santa Barbara. "You remember some guy here who owns a lawn service company...Tony Gomez? I don't know his exact involvement, but some cartel boys were driving his car when they hit Sharon Janson Zumadio...you remember the case?"

"You don't forget one who loses her head...particularly when the head's as pretty as hers was. You bet I remember, and I remember who smoked those guys—"

"You remember *a rumor* about who smoked those guys." I smile. He is a cop, after all.

"Right, *a rumor*. Anyway, you don't have to worry about Tony Gomez."

"Why's that?"

"He washed ashore down by Carpenteria...with a Columbian necktie."

I can't help but smile. "Made some of his compatriots angry, did he?"

"Guess so."

A Columbian necktie is when your throat is cut and the cutter drags your tongue out though the slit and watches you strangle to death on your own blood. Not a nice way to go, but in my opinion one fitting for this guy if he was involved in the death of my client.

"Good," I say, "one more scumbag, not only out of the tide pool, but out of the gene pool."

He agrees to introduce me to the detective, a guy named Sotomeyer, who worked the G5, and to meet me at Harry's in town at nine o'clock, and we part ways.

I've got time to kill, so I head into town to visit Samy's, one of my favorite toy stores—actually a sophisticated camera store—but I know they'll have the latest model of quadcopter with a built in GoPro camera. One came in very useful on my gig before last, and this one should be even more so as it comes with a monitor and you can see what it sees in real time, rather than having to download from a chip.

Then I wander downtown and enjoy being an ordinary guy, walking the streets, wandering in and out of shops, eyeballing the beautiful women, and trying to look normal. Tough as it is.

Heading back to Montecito, and still early, I stop at Lucky's, where the steaks are sixty bucks which helps keep out the riffraff like me. I have one glass of pinot grigio for what I'd normally pay for a bottle, and sip it for a half hour and watch the pretty people come and go. Then it's finally time to meet up with Wedgeworth.

Chapter Three

I guess there's been a shift change as there's a new no-neck at the gatehouse, this one a blond Germanic type who looks like he time-travelled right out of Hitler's SS. But he's polite, does the same gig with my license as the first one did, then calls up the main house and reassures himself that this guy Reardon in the 1957 Corvette is actually invited to the castle before he activates the electronic gates and I find myself on an excursion though a copse of oaks and eucalypti, all perfectly manicured.

And a castle it is. I know enough about Santa Barbara to know how they value their George Washington Smith designed mansions, and this is one, albeit one that appears to have been added onto a time or two since the 1920's, as wings on either side seem to be somewhat newer than the main structure. Altogether the Spanish themed residence has to be twenty thousand square feet, and I've covered twenty acres just winding my way up to the house.

My, the power of dot com dough. And this guy only in his late thirties.

Another no-neck awaits me, and he waves me around to the side entrance of the mansion.

I'm not surprised when he leads me to a servant's entrance.

We wind our way past an eight car garage holding a couple of million dollars in vehicles, then a pantry, a butler's pantry, through the kitchen, and out to a covered swimming pool. I'm seated at a table near a fifty inch built in TV and treated to a Monday night football game, but as soon as my butt hits the chair, a woman in maid's attire comes out and asks me what I'd like to drink, then informs me that Mr. Wedgeworth is tied up on a call and will join me shortly.

She heads out to get my Jack Daniels neat and as soon as she disappears, a young girl, trim and pretty with mouse-brown hair, with the nubbin breasts of a puberty child, in a modest bikini, exits another door and immediately does a graceful dive into the pool. She pops up as close as she can get to where I'm sitting ten feet from the edge.

"Hi," she calls out. "I'm Athena."

"Hi," I answer, and give her a smile and a nod. At first glance I figured her for her late teens, then, after she's spoken, adjust my opinion to early teen new to puberty.

"You here to see my dad?" she asks.

"If your dad is Prather Wedgeworth, I am."

"What's your name?"

"Mike."

"Hi, Mike."

"Hi, Athena."

"Friends call me Tenee."

"Tiny?"

"No, Tenee, no 'I', an 'E'."

"Nice to meet you, Tenee, if I can call you that."

Her smile suddenly fades.

"You shouldn't be bothering Mr. Reardon," an angry voice rings over my shoulder, and Wedgeworth strides to poolside, a beach towel in hand, and spreads it out, shielding my view of Tenee scrambling out of the pool. He wraps her in it and she hurries away, not looking back and heading back in the door she'd come out of.

He calls after her, "We'll have a talk later, young lady." Then he heads over and flops down across from me. "Sorry about that," he says.

"She's a pleasant young lady. No bother."

"She knows better than to interfere when I have business."

I shrug. She was hardly interfering by jumping into the pool, but I keep it to myself.

"Now," he says, "where were we?"

"Nowhere," I say, and see that he doesn't like that reply.

"I hardly think a half million is nowhere."

"At the risk of wondering if you heard me earlier, I might have to spend that much to get in a position to return your airplane. I'll have to hire a pilot and copilot—"

"What's the matter with using the people I have? Or can get?"

"Odds are your crew won't be up to this particular trip."

"Fact is," he says, his brow furrowed, "the old crew disappeared with the plane. I meant someone I'll hire who's new to the job."

"Odds are, I'll need someone who has military skills, and I don't mean just in the pilot and co-pilot seats."

"I see," he says, but looks a little puzzled.

We talk for over an hour, then finally agree on a two and a half million dollar fee. He agrees to advance fifty grand, and I assure him that I'll go through it quickly, and will have to come back to the trough for more. He assures me that I'll get more when and if I justify what

I've spent, against the total amount, of course. He makes it very clear it's an advance, not in addition to.

He finally extends his hand, and says, "I'll have my attorney—"

And I interrupt him. "Mr. Wedgeworth, I don't think you want to have a written agreement with me."

He looks a little surprised. "I don't enter into multi-million dollar agreements without having legal counsel."

"Then we've been talking for nothing. You don't want to know what I might have to do to get your airplane back. If you want an agreement, get a piece of note paper and write 'on the return of my G5 I agree to pay Mike Reardon two point five million bucks. You sign it and I will."

"So," he says, "you'll go to work on this without an agreement?"

"I'm not a bit worried about you paying me what we've agreed to, when I perform."

He laughs. "And what if I decide it's only worth a million, or three quarters of a million."

"You mean like you decided not to pay Henry Hausman the fee you'd agreed to pay?"

He noticeably reddens. "That's different. I'm not going to pay him. The plane was stolen on his watch."

I sigh deeply, and rise. "I'm not sure we can do business, Mr. Wedgeworth. If you say you'll pay me, I'll take you at your word. If I perform and you don't pay, then we have a problem, and I assure you that you don't want a problem with me. I always do exactly what I say I'll do, and I expect others to do so as well. Written agreements are merely fodder for attorneys."

He's looking a little too smug. Then he, too, rises. "I'll have a fifty thousand dollar check—"

"No check. Cash."

That takes him aback. "Cash, golly...."

"Yes, golly gee, cash."

His look sours. "Are you mocking me, Mr. Reardon?"

"No, sir, I think it's charming."

"I'll have a briefcase for you at the front gate by ten o'clock in the morning. Pick it up, then go get my airplane...and don't fail."

"I'll do my very best."

"Don't fail."

"I'll do my very best," I repeat. "And my best is as good as it gets."

He nods, takes his iPhone out of his pocket, and dials. As I stand and finish my drink, the no-neck, who'd walked me in, reappears.

Before I follow no-neck out, I turn to Wedgeworth. "I'll give this gentleman a cell phone that I'd appreciate you keep with you. It already has my number programmed in. It's as secure a line as we can get this day and age with big brother watching over everything we do. We don't want to talk many specifics on the cell, but it's good thing to have some line of communication other than phones easily traced to either of us."

"All James Bond stuff, eh?" he says.

"Hang onto it if you would."

"I will. Find my airplane," he says, gives me his back, and heads inside.

After giving no-neck a throwaway cell phone to give his boss, and noting the number in my cell, I am halfway back down the long drive, on a rather dark lane lit only by very small lights, when to my great surprise, the young lady I met at the pool steps out of the shadows, still in bikini with a matching see through wrap, and waves me down.

"You're out in the dark," I say, a little surprised.

"I hate my father," she says, pulling her wrap tighter in the chill.

"I'm sorry," I say, a little in shock.

"Nice wheels. Can you give me a ride into town?" she asks.

I'm struck dumb, and finally ask. "How old are you, Teene?"

"Fourteen. I need a ride to town."

"I can't do that, young lady. That would hardly be—"

"Then it's your fault."

"Sorry?" I say, more a question than a statement.

About that time, another pair of headlights appears a hundred yards back, and she fades back into the copse of trees.

I'm at a loss, but go ahead and hit the gas and head for the gates.

That was a bit of a mind blower, I think, as the gates open in front of me, and I turn back toward Santa Barbara, and head for Harry's Bar on the north end of State Street.

A mind blower.

Chapter Four

Harry's Bar, aka Harry's Plaza Café, is an institution in Santa Barbara, located in the crotch of a shopping center on upper State Street It's red leather booths and generous drinks embrace you with a warm welcome then leave you reeling if you have more than one of the bucket sized bombers they serve. Frickles—deep fried pickles—and deep fried ravioli will coat your arteries with enough cholesterol to keep your cardiologist happy and his Mercedes payments up to date.

And where else, in Santa Barbara, can you get Spaghetti al Burro or a Ranchero's rib-eye, and a beer, and still walk away with change from two Jacksons?

I love the place. It and Joe's Café on lower State Street—which used to be next to the Salvation Army—are a must for me in the beautiful city by the sea.

However, the look on the face of the guy sitting next to Ho-Man is giving me indigestion even before I reach the booth they occupy.

I stick out a hand and shake as Horace introduces me to Detective Allen Sotomeyer. He's slender, wrinkled cheap suit, with a slight pot belly and deep enough bags under gray eyes that he could pack for an extended trip to Europe. The guy looks like a much older and far more tired and terribly groomed George Stephanopoulos. And the groom-gods at SBPD have not called him aside of late as he has enough hair growing out of his ears and on and out of his rather bulbous vein-lined rosy nose that he's safe from an earwig invasion, as they could never broach the barrier. I guess there's some advantage to not giving a rat's ass how you look.

Both of them are well into Harry's bucket sized martinis, and I spot the barmaid, point to their drinks, and give her a thumbs up. She's a quick study and before we're finished with the niceties she's tableside and has a half-pint tumbler in front of me.

"So," Horace gets to the heart of the reason for our coming together, "Mike is working on the G5 thing, hired private by Wedgeworth, and would appreciate your help, Al."

The guy gives me a look like I've just pissed on his shoe, and with mouth turned down at the sides, asks, "So, Mike, what kind of brass do you carry?"

"I'm a bail enforcement officer, but other than that, I'm pure private."

He turns to Horace. "So, why the fuck should I make his life easy?"

"Because he's made mine easy a couple of times. And he could make yours easy some time, if he owed you a favor. And besides, he's buying the drinks."

"True," I say, and wait while Al makes up his mind.

Finally he sighs deeply and asks, "So, what do you want?"

I shrug. "What did your investigation turn up?"

"Fucking plane was missing for three days before it was called in. Wedgeworth's cousin was the pilot and in charge—"

"His *cousin*?"

"His cousin, and he's been missing along with the plane, as well as the co-pilot, who left a wife and two young kids out in Goleta."

"So, Vandenburg or some other radar installation must have tracked them?"

"They filed a flight plan to Hawaii, headed out that way, but never turned up there. I figured they swung south and are somewhere in South America where it's very tough to get information."

"Why South America?" I ask.

"Wedgeworth and his company, CalGeoCyber, had lots of business with several South American countries and lots of conflicts, so I'm thinking one of them got even with him."

"An interesting theory. Is it more than just a theory?"

"It's a fucking guess."

"What do you know about a guy named Henry Hausman?"

He gives a wry smile, then clears his throat and answers, "We just put a warrant out on him for trespassing and assault due to that bit out at Birnam Wood...which is one of the reasons I agreed to meet up with you as you're going to have to make a statement. It's not my gig, but one of the officers will be getting in touch."

Good fucking luck, I think, but don't say. "So who's Hausman?"

"Former head of security for CalGeoCyber and personally responsible for Wedgeworth's protection. I've met him a couple of times...seemed like a good guy, but he's being buried under the weight of billions...by the prick who fired him."

"How do I find the guy?" I ask.

"Hell, we want to find him and book him, so if you find him, advise."

I return the wry smile, and nod, but don't really mean it, at least not until I have a chat with the guy.

We talk for another half-hour, and he is kind enough to give me contact info on the pilot, co-pilot, and maintenance chief for the airplane. Then I pick up the tab for supper and bid my goodbyes.

As soon as I leave I text Wedgeworth and ask for a meeting. He comes right back and agrees to see me at ten a.m. when I'm supposed to pick up my fifty grand retainer, which may give me time in the morning to follow up on the leads I've gotten from Sotomeyer.

I get a cheap room, hit the sack early, get breakfast in the motel café, then promptly at eight a.m. call the crew chief's cell phone and find Fred Wilkerson, nickname 'Scoot', who's is now working for the avionics branch—Goleta Avionics—of the fixed base operator at the Santa Barbara airport and ask if I can see him in fifteen. He agrees. Then I call Mrs. Tobias Bartlett, wife of the co-pilot, explain that I've been hired to find the plane. Penny agrees to a cup of coffee at nine at the grammar school, Gaviota Elementary, where she is a secretary.

Fred 'Scoot' Wilkenson is a good guy for an ex-Air Force twerp. Solid, military cut hair, ebony eyes that look like they could laser-cut a sheet of aluminum aircraft skin, and a straight talker.

"Hell, I came to work and Sweet Sally...that's what the crew called her...was gone. She wasn't scheduled to be gone and I had some routine maintenance on the books. I called Mr. Wedgeworth's office as soon as I walked into an empty hangar and the girl said not to sweat it, so for three days I played catch up in the hangar on equipment, until I got another call telling me I was terminated along with my two guys. CalGeoCyber has a 414 as well, but they don't need full time maintenance on her…in fact I brought the account over here."

"Why was it three days before you got the boot?"

"I don't know. You know Glascock, the pilot—we called him bottle dick, as he drank way too much for a pilot and was a real dickhead—anyway, he is a cousin or some crap to Wedgeworth. I thought maybe the old boy stole Sweet Sally and Wedgeworth was hoping he'd bring her back from some joy ride somewhere."

I had to laugh and shake my head at that. "So, no idea where Sweet Sally might have ended up?"

"Not the foggiest."

"I was told Glascock filed a flight plan for Hawaii. Mechanical problems maybe—"

He takes umbrage at that, and bristles, "Bull shit, my planes don't have mechanical problems. My guess would be a swing south toward some country that doesn't pay much attention about their airspace, and that has to be south of Mexico."

"And the range of the G5?"

"Six thousand five hundred, and more with a skilled pilot. Hell, they could have made Lima, Peru if they didn't swing too far out to sea. We don't keep her topped off as there's no reason to carry the fuel if it's a domestic flight. But she was topped off the night they left."

"And Bartlett…the copilot?"

"Good kid. Straight shooter…he wouldn't be involved in anything fishy. I hope he's okay. He has a family."

I give Scoot a card with a cell phone number that will get to me, tell him I owe him a tall cold one, and take my leave.

Penny Bartlett is a pretty little thing with pictures of two kids on her gray metal desk in the outer office of the principal of Goleta Elementary. As soon as I introduce myself she leads me to a break-room down an exterior covered walkway. We have to thread our way through a bevy of recess rug monkeys on the way. The coffee is dishwater, as I suspected, but I appreciate her effort.

We sit across a folding picnic type table on metal folding chairs and she focuses on the coffee for a moment before raising her eyes and appraising me. Then tears well, and she sobs for a second before she dabs at her nose and eyes with a paper napkin, then collects herself.

"I'm sorry," I say, "if I'm bringing up what has to be a tough subject."

"I'll do anything...anything, to get Toby back here. Something is terribly wrong. I haven't heard a word from him, the plane's missing, and we need him home. He had the kind of job that he'd go to work, then call me from Tampa or someplace and say it would be a day or two...but he always, always, *always* called."

"You have no idea—"

"If I knew where he was, the kids and I would be going there."

"Anything ever said at home about this guy Glascock? I understand he was a boozer."

"Not at work, or Toby wouldn't have flown with him...even if he thought Charlie had a hangover."

"So you have no idea—"

"The plane has to have been stolen and Charlie and Toby kidnapped to fly it...or it crashed at sea during some unscheduled test flight...or something."

As I did with Scoot, I give her a card and my sympathies and walked her back to her office before heading to the parking lot.

Now it's time to have a little more in depth conversation with Wedgeworth. Before I fire up the

Vette, I text Pax and ask him to chase down CalGeoCyber's relationship with any South American countries and see if he can get a line on resultant trouble. I can hear his voice light up over the phone.

This is just the kind of gig he loves.

Chapter Five

Even though it's the same no-neck at the gate who was there the first time I charged the ramparts, I again have to show picture I.D. and he has to call before the gates to the inner-sanctum swing wide. As my retainer is supposed to be in a briefcase I ask, and he calls again, then hands it over. Being cautious, and with the top down on the Vette, I climb out and put it in the trunk.

It's a different no-neck who meets me and motions me around to the servants' entrance, then leads me through the eight-car garage and inside, only this time we find a butler's stairway leading up out of a pantry and ascend. I end up in an office that should have accommodated a half-dozen desks. Instead there's only one, befitting Napoleon, near a bank of windows overlooking rear grounds the size of a polo field.

Wedgeworth is reclined in a portable beauty salon type chair in a far corner, a washtub size plastic container of foot soak at his feet, with one foot in the lap of an attractive Hispanic lass and a hand being worked on by a girl who looks Vietnamese.

There's just something about a man getting a pedicure or even a manicure that makes my gut roll, but I maintain a straight face as he tells me to pull up a chair.

I dispense with the niceties. "You didn't mention the pilot was a relative."

"Oh, didn't I?"

"Was that why the delay in reporting the plane missing?"

"The plane was used by others in our company. You know our headquarters is out in Goleta near the university? I didn't know that they weren't off on business somewhere."

I think that's total bullshit, but charge forward. "And you failed to mention that you might have customers with some animosity toward you or the company...customers who may not only have ins with the police and military of some foreign countries, but may *be* the police or military?"

"And that's pertinent how?"

"I'm not an army, Mr. Wedgeworth. I can't invade a foreign country."

"Not my problem, Mr. Reardon. You took on a job, you have a retainer. I understand you picked the briefcase up on the way in."

I shrug. "I can always give it back."

"Golly, Mr. Reardon, what was all this stuff about man of your word, my word's my bond, a handshake is better than an agreement, no agreement necessary. What was all that?"

I can feel the heat creep up the back of my neck, because he's right. I take a deep breath. "Mr. Wedgeworth, I always do what I say I'm going to do, and when and if I don't you'll know I'm pushing up daisies. So, yes, I'll go get your airplane, if it's not crashed and on the bottom of the Pacific. But I need a little cooperation. Who in your company would be best to talk with about which clients have a hard-on for CalGeoCyber—"

"Geeze, Mike, there are ladies here," he whispers, and the two girls working on him giggle.

"Sorry. If you can't, or won't, who can tell me who's most likely to have it in for CalGeoCyber?"

"In-house counsel. Norval Blumenthal. He handles all the legal matters. We'll let him know you're coming." He turns to the girl doing his nails. "Kim, please ask Tatya to step in." The girl runs to a walnut paneled side door, sticks her head through, and she's followed back into the room by a five foot eight inch blond in a beautifully tailored dark suit with a red scarf tucked into a plunging neckline and I wish away the scarf as it's occluding the view. Six inch stiletto heels bring her up to my height. Her legs are bare, as is the fashion, and it's tanned legs like hers that set that pace. She cuts ice blue eyes at me, but only a glance.

"Yes, Mr. Wedgeworth?"

"This is Mike Reardon. He's helping us with the G5. Will you take him into your office and arrange for him to meet with Blumenthal." Then he turns back to me. "Good luck." He turns back to her. "Walk him out when you're done, via the outside hallway, please." And he goes back to the important work of perfect finger- and toenails.

I follow the blonde out into an adjoining office, and wish I could follow her all afternoon as she's a joy to behold from the back as well as from the front. As soon as the door closes, she turns to me and extends a beautifully manicured hand. "Hi. I'm Tatya, Mr. Wedgeworth's personal secretary. Have a seat and make yourself comfortable while I call the office."

So I do, and as soon as I do, another door opens, and a brunette, this one pretty but a little shop-worn with hair slightly askew, sticks her head in. "Tatya, get me a driver for this afternoon." She sees me and then steps inside and walks over, and as the blonde dials, sticks out her hand, with a diamond thereon that makes me blink as it catches the morning sun through the windows behind the blonde's desk. I jump up and take her hand as she says, "I'm Portia Wedgeworth."

"Hi, Mike Reardon."

"You're here to see Tatya."

"Mr. Wedgeworth, actually."

"About?" she asks, with a nice smile, but I catch the whiff of bourbon on her breath, and it's way shy of eleven in the morning.

"About his asking me to come meet with him," I say, my smile a little tight. I don't talk about a client's business, even with his or her spouse.

"My," she says, her eyes narrowing a little, even though she keeps the smile pasted on, "aren't you the evasive one."

"No, ma'am, just respecting good business practice."

The smile fades and she interrupts Tatya, who's now talking on the phone. "Forget the driver, I'll drive myself."

As she heads for the door, Tatya calls out to her. "Do you think that's a good—"

Portia, the wife, flips a middle finger over her shoulder, and I turn back to the blonde, acting as if I didn't see. She noticeably flushes, then goes back to the phone and hangs up. "I'm sorry for her behavior," she says.

I shrug. "So, Mr. Blumenthal?" I ask.

"He'll see you as soon as you can get there or anytime this afternoon."

"Thanks, Tatya." And I can't help myself, as I'm bound to be spending some time around Santa Barbara. "So, I can't help but notice, no ring on your left hand."

She flashes a gleaming smile. "It's not always admired these days...wearing a wedding ring, I mean."

"So, that means you're married, or not married?"

She eyeballs me a second, and I'm happy to say I feel I'm being undressed, then says, "Not, but this is neither the time nor place to discuss personal things."

"And where might be the time or place."

She laughs. "I hang out at Lucky's occasionally, and sometimes at the piano bar at the Biltmore."

"And tonight?"

She hesitates a moment, looks me up and down, then offers, "If I would happen to run into someone I met while at work, it couldn't ever, ever, ever get back to Mr. Wedgeworth."

"I hear Lucky's has the best steak in Santa Barbara, and I'm dying for some protein."

"Who knows, I might be there, but we never quit around here until after eight...at least we worker bees don't."

"Then buzz over to Lucky's about eight. I'll be there."

"Maybe," she says, with a teasing tone that says yes, then waves me to follow and walks me down the hall, down a back stairway, and to the Vette.

"Oh!" she says, "I love these old cars. I wanted one so much when I was growing up in Poland."

"And you have no accent," I say.

She laughs, waves, and disappears back into the eight car garage.

I hang a right onto East Valley and notice a steel gray Mercedes SL550, a fine ride, that had been parked a half block back from the entrance to the estate. I watch it pull out and gun it until it's only a car length behind.

And she's waving at me.

Chapter Six

I'm tempted to ignore her, as I know nothing good can come of this. First it was the daughter who waved me over, now the mother.

There's a small shopping center with a market and restaurant a half block ahead, and I'm thinking of turning into the parking lot, when she zooms up beside me and yells, "Pull over into the lot."

And I do so, and park, and she pulls in beside me. I glance at my watch and see it's now just twenty to eleven. She leaps out of the little hundred grand plus Mercedes sports car and climbs in beside me.

"I want to talk to you," she says, and it's not a request, it's a demand.

"Yes, ma'am," I say, in my most differential tone. "Talk away."

"No, in the bistro."

I shrug. What harm can a talk in a bistro be? I look up and see it's a 'wine bistro. It's located where an Italian restaurant was the last time I was here. I hesitate, but she jumps out and starts walking.

"They won't be open," I call out.

Without turning back, she says, "They'll open for me. They're there, getting ready for lunch."

I follow, and for some reason, I feel I'm walking toward the edge of a cliff.

She bangs on the door, waits until I catch up, then bangs again. The door opens a crack and some young lady says, "We open in a half hour."

But Portia Wedgeworth is not to be refused. She pushes the door hard enough that the young girl in a waitress's apron stumbles back.

"You're open," Portia says, and charges on by.

I hesitate, and she spins and demands, "Get in here, Reardon."

I hear the young girl say as we pass, "Oh, Mrs. Wedgeworth, I didn't know it was you."

She moves on through the foyer and out onto a patio, then flops down in a wire chair. The girl follows closely. "Would you like a pinot grigio?" she asks.

"When are you going to get some friggin' booze in this claptrap?" Portia snaps.

"Sorry, ma'am, still no hard liquor license."

"Yes to the pinot. Bring a bottle and two glasses."

I'm beginning to get a little disgusted with Mrs. Wedgeworth, but it is a two-and-a-half-million-dollar fee, so I bite my lip and park my butt across from her. She is a beautiful woman, if a little rough around the edges, and a tad puffy, probably from the booze. If she's the same age as her husband, she can't be forty yet. She merely sits and stares me down until the girl arrives with the bottle and glasses. She starts to pour but Portia grabs the bottle out of her hands.

"We don't need you anymore until this bottle is empty." She fills both glasses far beyond the proper widest spot where the wine would breathe the most, then gives me a quick nod as if that's a good thing.

"Yes, ma'am," the girl says, backing away, and it's obvious she's happy to get out of Portia's gun-sights. She spins on a heel and hurries back inside.

"So, Mikey, what was your business with my husband?"

"Sorry, Mrs. Wed—"

"Portia, if you don't mind."

"Portia, I'm in the sub rosa business, and those of us who are, are not there for long if we talk about our clients." She starts to snap at me, but I stop her with an extended palm out. "And I will not divulge my business with a client unless specifically instructed to do so by that client."

"It's half my money," she growls.

"That's for you to know, but I'm not privy to what's what or even who's who and certainly not to your marital arrangements...and have no interest in being so."

Her look hardens. "Is he paying you to follow me?"

I laugh at that. "Mrs. Wedgeworth, I don't involve myself in domestic disputes, even one as interesting as the one you're involved in might be. It's a business thing, not a personal one."

"Then," she says, this time her voice much softer, "it has to be his fucking cousin and that airplane."

He's a gee-and-golly guy, and she's a fuck-this fuck-that kind of girl. "Can't say if it is or isn't."

"Okay then, drink up. We'll talk about something else...something more pleasant."

Again I laugh, as she downs the whole glass of wine and reaches for the bottle while I take a sip.

Her voice goes another octave lower. "How about we go somewhere that we can get a real drink."

So I lie. "You have no idea how much I'd enjoy that, but I have an appointment that your husband set up for me, and I'm already late."

She leans back in the chair, takes a long look, and finally asks, "You don't like me, do you?" She actually pouts a lip out enough that a sparrow could perch there.

I chuckle a little sardonically. "Mrs. Wedgeworth, I don't know you well enough to form an opinion." Then comes the lie. "On the surface you certainly seem nice enough."

"Liar. If you got to know me better...lots better, you'd see how lovable I could be." I didn't think it possible, but she pouts even more.

And she stresses *lovable*. I smile, drink down half my wine, and rise. "Got to go. Hope we can do this again some time." It's all I can do not to run for the door.

"Fucking A," she says, under her breath.

And I head for the door into the restaurant. The girl is working behind the nearby bar, and I walk over. "What do I owe you for the wine?" I ask.

"One twenty," she says, and I'm pretty sure she doesn't mean a buck twenty. I peel out a Franklin and two Jacksons and hand them over. "Keep the change," and head for the door and am gone.

"Thanks," I hear her call out behind me.

Now to find out who might want to hurt CalGeoCyber and Prather K. Wedgeworth fifty mil worth, then kill enough time to check out Lucky's and, hopefully, the Polish side of life.

Mrs. Wedgeworth is one thing to be avoided like the proverbial plague, but Tatya is another...and who knows what a guy might learn from a girl who probably knows most of her employer's secrets?

Chapter Seven

Norval Blumenthal has an office on the ground floor of the three-storey building that's CalGeoCyber. His office has a window wall opening onto a private garden full of orchids, which grow too easily on California's Central Coast. The only smile I get out of him is when I compliment him on the garden. He's got a high forehead and an oversized skull, at least it appears to be, and by the ego wall behind his desk, it's packed full of a well-exercised brain. He's very quick; he finishes about half my sentences for me, as if he's in a hurry to get back to work.

He carefully does not go into specifics about the company's business, or any lawsuits wherein they are the defendant, but the gist of it is that CalGeoCyber worked for a half dozen South American countries setting up a variety of systems, both software and hardware, some of which were so secret that they had to train people from those countries to do the work, and they could not be privy to the information. Much of that didn't work out to well, as they continue to battle several lawsuits—which he admits to after I remind him that lawsuits are public filings—from countries who want a couple of hundred million refunded. The primary problems, he finally relates, are with Ecuador and Paraguay. So my investigation will start there. Or, I should say, my buddy Pax's investigation will start there when I forward the info to him.

As soon as I leave, I check my phone and see I have a text message from Pax, with instructions to find a place where I can print off some files from email and do so.

Paxton Weatherwax and I served together in Desert Storm, both ending up as warrant officers, and I went into a hot firefight to drag him out of harm's way when he'd taken one from an AK47 through the thigh, a leg that is now an inch shorter than the other. He repaid the favor, dragging a leg with his thigh splinted with fence boards and wearing a field dressing, when I was so rummy from a nearby RPG that I was on my feet and wandering around, a duck in a shooting gallery, like I'd just put down a fifth of Jack Daniels. After that, we put down many together, until I was relieved of duty and mustered out with a General Courts-martial, thanks to poking double-ought buck holes in a half dozen *Hajis* who were stoning a couple of young ladies—young ladies who were members of their own families. It was partially my fault, as they were caught in what was considered by the Iraqis to be an intimate situation and I would consider a public conversation—which in fact, is what it was.

The world is full of injustice and, unfortunately, much of it stems from religious belief.

Anyway, Pax and I are about as close as two guys can get without being swishy. And yes, both of us would go the route for the other, no matter the odds.

I'm fortunate to have a buddy who left the corps and became an Internet Provider. He can route messages to me through a hundred small black boxes in as many cities around the world. Thus, I remain under the radar. He can also move what small sums of money I earn in ways that defy explanation.

I print off a half a ream of information gathered by my cyber-savvy buddy Pax, and find a bench near the beach where I'm only distracted by a half dozen college girls playing volleyball in their bikinis. And a distraction it is! After reading the afternoon away, my attention is centered on General Hector Maldonado, who is very high up in the Paraguayan Air Force as a result of an article, which I can't read as it's in Spanish, in the Asuncion, Paraguay newspaper, *La Nacion*. It seems he is in possession of a beautiful new business aircraft, variety unnamed, but one that will seat sixteen, and the paper has taken umbrage, as it's not one manufactured in neighboring Brazil. The G5 is the only other business aircraft that would fill that bill—seating that many, and non-Brazilian manufactured.

It seems I'm taking a trip to Paraguay. My last act before heading for Lucky's, hopefully to get lucky, is to text Pax and ask him to find me someone in Paraguay we can trust who'll act as guide and interpreter.

Just in case I might have a fortunate turn of events, I rent one of the small rooms at the Montecito Inn next door to Lucky's, and clean up. I've got to have a place to sleep and I need one more morning on the coast as I haven't done any investigation into Charles Bottle-Dick, as Scoot referred to him. Someone must know more about Glascock than I've learned so far.

I'm perched on a bar stool promptly at eight p.m. properly attired in black jeans, a maroon button down shirt, stylish Montecito-playboy loafers, and a black silk and wool blazer. And by the time I have a Jack Daniels neat in front of me, beautiful blond Tatya enters. She's even taller on black stelitto heels that look impossible, but she makes them look easy. A brilliant electric blue silk blouse follows and clings to every curve. Lycra, or some expandable material for the black pants, leaves little to be discovered—not that they don't encourage me to try. She turns every head in the bar—men with hungry hound dog I-wanna-lick-you-all-over looks and women with tight-lipped cobra glares—and I'm not surprised when the bartender greets her by name, and she him. The dozen seats at the bar are full of Montecito's other pretty people, but a nook in the back has one table unoccupied. I pick up my drink as soon as she walks over and lead her back there.

"So, you made it," she says, flashing a smile showing either God-given perfect teeth or about a ten grand investment.

"I did...you don't think I'd miss an opportunity to get to know the most beautiful woman in Montecito."

"That's quite a statement as there are dozens, maybe hundreds, of beautiful women near here."

"I have a very discerning eye, and seldom exaggerate."

"You're too kind, sir."

"So, Polish?" I ask, as a conversation starter as we park ourselves across a small table.

"Yes, and I've heard all the Polish jokes," she says, with a knowing smile.

"I haven't. Do you know some?"

"A thousand or so, and I've filed them all in my circular file next to my desk."

I laugh. "And rightfully so. So, what does Tatya do, other than serve Master Wedgeworth?"

"I paint a little, I play some violin, and I walk and sometimes run on the beach."

"You are obviously fit, so you must do a lot of beach walking or running."

"We have a gym at the estate, and I occasionally...well, daily to tell the truth...work out there. I had a visitor this afternoon, full of questions about the handsome Mr. Reardon."

"The visitor's words, or yours?" I ask.

"Oh, the visitor's...I never judge so quickly being a believer that beauty is truly only skin deep." The barmaid sidles up beside her and she orders a Manhattan, up, then turns back to me. "So, do your good looks only go skin deep, or are you more than a pretty face?"

That makes me laugh. "Pretty is something I've never been accused of being. I've got enough scars on my mug you'd think I was a professional hockey player, and if you could see the rest of me you'd think I've been through a meat grinder—"

"All honorably earned, I hope," she says, and reaches over and traces one over my eyebrow, a fairly fresh one from having a half dozen assholes go after me with bats and pipes during my last gig in Williston, North Dakota.

"I hope," I say. "Honor is high on my list."

"Military, I'll bet?"

"Marine Corps, Recon if you know what that is...Desert Storm...and a few other interesting places, most of which I can't talk about."

"Scars on a man give him character, and character is almost always way more than skin deep."

My curiosity finally niggles at me, and since she hasn't offered, I ask, "So, who was curious about Mr. Reardon?"

"Mrs. Wedgeworth, but she probably won't remember as she came in at five...and I shouldn't say this...but soused as usual."

We talk through two drinks, supper, and two after-dinner drinks, then have another at the tiny bar next door in the Montecito Inn. There never seems to be a question that she's going to the room with me, so I don't ask. When we leave, we cross the driveway, and I usher her into the hotel, the elevator, the small but expensive room, and, I hope, into a state of total sexual satiation.

And yes, she's very fit, and I'm glad I am, too, as I had to spend half the night making sure satiation was the order of the evening.

I'm not used to having a lady slip out while I'm asleep, but she managed to do so.

And I hate that fact, as I wanted to finish a couple more things with the long legged blonde. One was to ply her for info on the Wedgeworth cousin and pilot, and two was to enjoy prying, or should I say pumping, a little information out of her just one more time before she slipped away. Even after a night like I had, I awake with my pry-bar at attention and ready for a rematch.

Who'd a thunk it?

Chapter Eight

My message light is blinking—I'd asked the desk to hold my calls—and I find a nice missive recorded thereon from Tatya, who tells me she had to get home to feed her cats then get a few hours' sleep before getting up for work. I have to smile when she tells me that she's left instructions in the Montecito Café in the hotel, which is a place I enjoy, and is buying my breakfast even though she can't be there. She also is kind enough to leave her cell phone number and email address.

A good sign of a job well done.

As soon as I step out of the shower, my cell chimes and it's *Ring of Fire*, which means it's my buddy Pax.

He never bothers with hello, so it's, "You'll never guess?"

"Test me," I reply.

"I've found you an interpreter, and way better."

"How so?"

"Name, Carmen Fabriana Diaz; former employer, Rubén Marcos Valasquez, and you'll never guess who Ruben is."

"Never in a million years."

"The Consulate General of Paraguay in Los Angeles. Carmen is a Paraguayan citizen who speaks perfect

English...not that you understand most English...and is looking for employment."

"And is fat and smartass, I'm sure, which I know is what you'd hire for me, given the chance?"

"I'll let you be the judge."

"So, how did you find Miss Carmen Fabulous?"

"Fabriana...Diaz. And I found her on the net, of course. She was on Linkedin looking for a position."

"How do I get together with Miss Fabulous?"

"I gave her your cell and she's calling you mid-morning and wants to meet with you somewhere on your way back to Vegas...if you're coming back to Vegas? I'll also text you her number."

"I am heading your way, to plot and plan with you and see if I can get Skip to stand by in case...as soon as I do just a little more groundwork here. By the way, see what you can dig up on Mrs. Portia Wedgeworth, who seems to be a lush, and on Tatya Bolinsky, who's Prather's personal secretary and works out of his home office."

"Will do."

"By the way, what was Carmen's job at the Consulate?"

"Cultural Attaché, and you know what that probably means."

"Yeah. If it means the same thing it does in our embassies, she's a spy."

"She didn't fess to it during our talk, but didn't deny it either."

After a nice light breakfast, going easy on Tatya's pocketbook, I drive out to Goleta to check out the nice three bedroom tract house belonging to G5 pilot, and cousin, Charles Glascock. On the way, I stop at a florist and send Tatya a dozen red roses, card unsigned with merely a note, 'thanks for breakfast'.

There are a half-dozen newspapers in the Glascock driveway, even though there's a Dodge pickup parked there. I park in front, make my way to the door, and use the bell a few times, then rap loud enough to wake the neighbors.

No answer, no sign of life, so I peer in the window—hard to do as the drapes and blinds are shut—and see a pile of mail in the entry under the mail slot in the door. I decide there's a slight chance there's a lead there, so I return to the Vette and dig a set of picks out of the trunk. Eyeballing the neighboring houses for lookieloos, and not seeing anyone, I find a side-yard gate and then a Hollywood kitchen door. It would be much easier to just break the glass and turn the handle as there's no dead bolt, but being a good citizen I go ahead and invest five minutes with picks and then swing the door aside.

I stop short with my foot still in the air on stepping in, as I hear some scraping sound in the distance. I listen for a moment, then think it must have been my imagination, or that it could have come from outside and been a dog or cat or something.

Heading for the front door, across a kitchen then though a darkened front-facing dining room with its drapes pulled tight, I kneel by the pile of mail in the entry and begin sorting through it. Then things spin like hell and I find myself tumbling back into the dining room, landing flat on my back, my head swimming.

I'm a dumb shit. Obviously the sound was someone not something.

A shape is charging me, and I roll to my stomach and launch myself under the dining room table. Knocking chairs out of the way on the other side, I come up as a very big guy dives over the top of the table and clips me one on the chin—thank God I see it coming and slip the punch enough that it only knocks me off balance and up against the wall, but he, too, is trying to get his feet under him.

I bounce off the wall and back into him with an overhand right followed by a hard uppercut left to his midsection, but's he's no pansy and pounds me with a couple of roundhouses as he's coming upright.

I slip the third roundhouse. Missing, he spins halfway around and, quartering behind him, I catch him with a straight right on the jaw joint. He goes to one knee, but he's still not through and plunges forward, trying a double leg takedown, but I post off his head with my left hand, shoving him down while bringing three hard rights to the side of his head. High school and college wrestling comes in handy again.

He sags, and I back away, trying to figure out who the hell this is in the dim light, and catch a heel on one of the chairs I've knocked over coming out from under the table. I spin as I go down so I'll have my hands in front, land in a push up position and spring to my feet, but he's on my back, and gets a death grip on my neck with his right arm while trying to get to the Glock in its holster in the center of my back with his left, all while trying to sink his right forearm deep so he can choke me out.

While I fight with one hand to keep him away from my pistol, I grapple with the other for my only recourse which is to pry away and try and break a finger. I get hold of his index finger and break his grip on my neck.

He lunges forward, following the finger that I'm twisting like hell, and makes the mistake of leaning his chin on my shoulder. I throw my midsection forward, keeping him away from the pistol at the same time I reach back, secure a hand behind his neck, and kick my legs out from under myself. throwing my full weight and dragging him down, then spin as I go. I can actually hear his neck wrench and pop as I go to my belly, then regain my feet. He's on his face on the floor, moaning.

"You broke my fucking neck," I can hear from his face planted in the carpet.

"I tried like hell," I say, as I go over and fling the drapes open. "Well, Henry Hausman, as I live and breath," I say, enjoying the fact he's face down and I'm still breathing.

He manages to roll to his back, both hands on his neck, trying to determine if he's going to be a paraplegic, and mumbles, "Fuck, that was a good move."

"Thanks, Henry." He's still on his back. "Are you carrying?" I ask.

"What do you think?" he says, still rubbing his neck with both hands.

"Roll to your belly so I can retrieve your weapon, as I know from experience that's where you carry. And no bullshit or I'll stomp the back of your sore neck and if it's not broken, it will be."

"I'm through. Take the frickin' gun."

He does as instructed, and I take the frickin' gun.

"Can you get up?" I ask.

"Yeah, I'm getting some feeling back."

"Then take a seat and let's have a talk."

"There's a couple of beers in the refrigerator."

"Too early for me. Sit."

He moves slowly, getting to his feet, and settles into a chair at the far end of the table.

"So, what the hell are you doing here?" I ask.

Chapter Nine

He takes a deep breath, and winces as he continues to rub his neck, then talks.

"I knew the locals would be hunting me after that debacle at Birnam Wood, and I knew this asshole pilot wasn't using this place, as I'd checked it out when I was still on Wedgeworthless's payroll. It was a good place to lay low, and the price was right...particularly after that prick cousin of Glascock's didn't honor his agreement and pay me the bonus I had coming."

"Why'd he can you?"

"Because his fucking cousin flew away in his airplane, that's why. Like I could have anticipated that move...that and he thinks I diddled his old lady, which I didn't do. He owes me the dough, nonetheless, and owed it to me two months before his plane departed."

I have to nod, as that's the way I understood it. "So, how'd you get a security job with him?"

"I've worked security for ten years after I got out of Delta Force, two for Wedgeworth. Not much else for a guy to do whose first reaction is to tear someone's head off. We make piss poor real estate or insurance salesmen."

That makes me laugh. "I know the feeling, Marine recon myself. I need to know how to get hold of you, in case I have a job for you...after I check you out, that is."

"I damn sure need the work. I've got an ex-wife and two kids back in Kansas City and a fifty thousand dollar judgment to pay off for breaking some asshole's jaw who was trying to nail Wedgeworthless...and you don't think that prick would pay, do you?"

"You got a cell number?" I ask.

"No, I chucked it into the bird refuge when I knew the cops wanted to have a long talk with me."

"Good thinking. I've got a throwaway in the car and will give you one."

"What's the job?"

"Kicking ass, same old crap for you and me."

"That I know how to do."

"Any ideas about this G5?" I ask.

He gives me a hard look, then smiles. "It's Hank, by the way, nobody calls me Henry if they want to live. The G5? After I'm on the payroll."

I have to laugh again. I'm starting to like him.

I pop the clip on his 9mm Springfield semi-auto, eject the shell from the chamber, flip the clip into a far corner and the weapon to him. Which he deftly catches. "Follow me out to get the phone," I say, "and don't bother picking up the clip until I'm gone."

"No sweat," he says.

Now to tie up with Miss Carmen Fabulous Diaz.

I hated to go all the way back to Vegas, but there were a few things I had to pick up from my mini-storage there. Not everything I would need in Paraguay, I'm sure, as most of what I might need I couldn't get on any commercial flight.

I maintain mini-storage spaces in three cities: Las Vegas, Nevada; Ventura, California; and Sheridan, Wyoming. And they are not just for storing the normal crap a normal person collects. As I don't maintain an apartment, these ministorage units are all that tie me to the world, as most folks know it. I did acquire a Ford 250 and Lance camper last year, a big step for me as it smacks of a taste of being a homebody, but it's totally portable so it's not much of a taste. I still sleep in the ministorage units upon occasion.

In addition to the bug-out bag I keep in my van, and the mini-version thereof in the narrow storage bins on the back of my Harley, I have major ones in each storage room and the whole camper now is a bug-out bag. With any of the major bug-out bags, and even without the camper, I could live in the Rockies, the Sierras, or the deserts for a long, long time, if not forever, without the benefit of cities. If you can call cities a benefit.

I've accumulated a nice collection of weapons, and they are widely distributed among secret side panels in the van and in hideouts in the three storage rooms, and I'm slowly finding places to create hideouts in the camper. On casual observation, you see no weapons in any of my facilities. In each storage room I have an upright armoire size cabinet with hidden weapon storage. Both ends swing open with hidden push latches to reveal four long arms in each. Drawers under what appear to be three inch thick shelving hold ammunition, side arms, and other accouterments. The shelves are covered with clothes and other mundane items to make the armoire look as if that's its purpose.

I try to stay as close to a one man army as one man can.

Getting the itch to say goodbye to the beautiful Tatya, it's all I can do not to turn off on Hot Springs Road and head up to East Valley Road and the Wedgeworth estate, but as promised, I'll not give my new client any inkling that I know Miss Tatya more than to give a casual wave.

But I pass the turnoff with some niggling in my loins. And just as I do, my phone gives me a generic ring, and I look at, to my pleasure, the Wedgeworth residence calling...ask, I think, and ye shall receive. There's a Bluetooth earpiece in the ashtray of the Vette and I center it in my ear, hit the little receive button, and give who I hope is Tatya a howdy.

"Mike," the voice on the other end says, and it's not Tatya's.

"You got him," I say.

"This is Tenee."

"Who?"

"Athena Wedgeworth. You remember, we talked at the pool then you stiffed me for a ride down the drive—"

"Sure, kid, how are you?"

"Freakin'."

I have to pause for a moment, then ask, "Okay, what's freakin' you?"

"My dad, and my mom. Can I hire you?"

That makes me smile. Then I ask, "For what?"

"I have to get Venee...that's my little sister, Venus...Venee...and I out of here."

"Athena—"

"I hate that name, call me Tenee."

"Tenee, I'm working for your dad on a job that could make me a lot of money. I can't jeopardize that...besides, it would be a conflict of interest." Then I hesitate, and ask, "So, what's the problem?"

"If I can't hire you, I can't tell you."

"Don't you have a little brother also?"

"Yes, but he's not...he's not in trouble?"

"What kind of trouble?"

"I can't tell you."

"Then I can't help you."

"You said you couldn't help anyway...so it doesn't matter."

"Look, I'll be back in a week or two, and that should finish my business with your dad. Then we'll talk."

"That may be too long, but if I'm still here, then we can talk."

I'm at a loss, so I sigh, and say, "We'll talk then."

I hear a slight catch in her voice, and wonder if she's crying. Odds are ninety nine to one that it's some teenage bullshit like the old man's going to take her phone away, so I repeat, "We'll talk then," but she hangs up without replying.

Whatever it is, it's got to go on the back burner. So I call Pax and get him to call my potential translator and set up a meet.

In moments he calls back with a location, a Marie Callenders restaurant on the Magic Mountain Parkway turnoff in Valencia in an hour. I can just make it, and it's a perfect spot as it's only about a hundred yards out of my way.

But, being a man meeting up with a woman he's never met before, I have to ask, "So, is she a looker?"

He laughs. "The job is translation, remember. Looks to me, from the Linkedin picture, she's from a long line of tortilla eaters and mama made them with pure lard, but it was a head shot."

"Okay, other than a generous frame, how do I recognize her?"

"She said blue blouse, blue jeans, long black hair."

"Okay, I'm on my way."
I am close to heading out to Paraguay.

Chapter Ten

I don't have to look far as she's on a bench near the door, reading an international edition of the Wall Street Journal. At first glance, with her still seated, I can see that she hasn't spent much time knocking down lard-based tortillas. She looks solid, not fat; not svelte, but curvaceous. She's probably a head shorter than I, but she makes up for some of it with five inch high heels. Her hair is long, to the middle of her back, and raven-wing-black and bright as a new black Mercedes. She has gray eyes, smoked glass, deep, and mysterious. Bright red lipstick and nails are an interesting contrast. A tightly bound blue scarf, matching her silk blouse, in place of a belt, is threaded through her belt loops in jeans that look like they were painted on over the flare of hips. No hint of chubby. She's solid, curvy, and very interesting, easy on the eye.

"You're Mr. Reardon?" she asks, folding the paper carefully and putting it aside before rising. She extends a hand, and shakes. She has only the hint of a Hispanic accent.

"Guilty," I reply, taking the hand. "And you're Carmen." I like women with a firm handshake.

"Got time for a cup of coffee?" she asks.

"You bet." And we easily find a seat in the middle of the afternoon, between lunch and supper.

She orders coffee, and I do the same plus a piece of apple pie...after all it is Marie Callendars.

She gets right down to business. "I speak Spanish, of course, German, Portuguese, and Guarani—"

"Whoa, what the hell is *Guaraní*?"

"So, you've never been to *Corazón de America*? The heart of America...of course, you'd say South America."

"I've been around Mexico some and Central America, a short gig in Columbia, and spent a couple of days in Rio, but that's it."

"Okay, so *Guaraní* are the indigenous people of Paraguay. Almost all Paraguayans are bilingual and speak that original language as well as Spanish. We're the only country who's maintained our heritage in that regard."

The coffee and pie arrives and I take a bite before continuing. Then ask, "So, you were employed by your consulate...a good job, I'd think. Why leave?"

"I had a little disagreement with the not-so-nice vice-counselor general, who still clings to the old ways."

"Which means?"

"After two wars in the eighteen hundreds Paraguay's population was decimated. We lost as many as seventy five percent of our population, and almost all our male population. Polygamy was common, and necessary, and even overlooked by the church."

"Which means?"

"May I be frank?"

"Do I look like a guy who minces words?"

She laughs, then says, "The son of a bitch wouldn't keep his hands off me and I finally kicked him in the *huevos*. He fired me, and tried to send me home, but I have a work visa from the U.S., outside of the embassy's control. A precaution I took, as I was determined not to be his *puta*, yet wanted to work in the States."

I'm starting to like, and gain respect for the lady.

She knows what she wants, and charges forward.

"I don't work cheap," she says.

"So, what's 'not cheap?"

"Two thousand a week and you pick up all expenses."

"You're right, that's not cheap. I was thinking more like a grand a week—"

"You're going to Paraguay, right?"

"Yes, ma'am."

"And I know the language, have relatives there, and I know a half-dozen senators, the *presidente*, and a handful of generals as well as those powerful in industry and banking. I should be asking for five thousand a week."

"What's your family do?"

"Farms, primarily soy beans. But some corn and coffee too."

"So, they grow soy beans in...how'd you call it... *Corazón de America,* the heart of America?"

"We're the fourth largest producer of soy beans in the world."

"Okay, fifteen hundred a week."

"Do you have a visa? ...That can take months. I can get you one in an hour."

"Okay, okay, two grand a week."

"I'm paid weekly, on Friday, in cash. And a month guarantee?"

"You're a hard woman, Carmen Fabriana Diaz."

"It's a hard country. And looking at you, I doubt if you're going to my country to pick up knickknacks. Right?"

"I'm not much for knickknacks. I'm going down to retrieve some stolen property...can you handle that?"

"I don't believe in stealing, so I can get behind that, as you Americans say. You may be leaving the country without me, so long as you understand I have no interest in a vacation in Pacumbu High Security Prison. Women are a little too welcome there...the guards and the bull dykes would love me."

"I'll bet...if the women look like you. My buddy has your number. I'll call in the morning and tell you our schedule. When can you go to work?"

"As soon as we shake hands, I'm on the payroll."

Again, I laugh. "Okay, let's not shake until I'm ready to drive away."

Now it's her turn to laugh, and she does it very attractively and demurely, dropping her eyes and head, looking up like a coquette. "I'll need your passport number to get that visa."

"I'll call from Vegas. Be ready to go on a moment's notice."

"*No hay problema, señor. Hasta mañana.*"

"*Por la mañana.* You an early riser?"

"When I have to be. Otherwise I curl up like a cat in the sun."

"*Gato del sur.* I'll put the call off until seven."

"*Gata*, thank you very much. And it's *sol*, not *sur*. *Sur* is the south. I can see this is going to be a contentious relationship." She frowns at me, but it quickly turns to a smile. She's teasing.

"Not unless you want to charge extra for the Spanish lessons. Do your work, don't whine...but then I can picture you growling, but not whining."

That gets a flashing smile from the lady. "I'll pull my weight."

I smile, grab the ticket, motion toward the door, and wait for her to rise and lead the way.

As we head for the cashier, she asks, "So, what got stolen?"

"We'll talk some about it on the plane...you're better off not knowing. I'll expect an education on Paraguay."

"I'm just the girl who can do it. First class, I hope."

"Not normally, but I plan to go under the cover of a successful business man, so first class it is."

"I'll be packed. Let's shake so we can get the meter running."

"A hard, hard woman."

Chapter Eleven

Pax's office is a simple two-storey affair with a storefront facing a parking lot. The former beauty shop in the storefront has had the windows whitewashed with only the glass door remaining clear, and the small gold lettered sign announces Weatherwax Internet Services. He has six employees on site, and offices in three other cities. Consultants number of another dozen in India and the Philippines who do contract work for him. His personal office is the size of a two-car garage and located second storey rear, with a great view of the strip in the distance, were he ever to open the drapes on his wide window. They normally remain closed, as the room sports at least a dozen monitors, one of which spreads at least fifty inches. The server room is next to his office, and in air-conditioned splendor are a half-dozen mysterious boxes as tall as myself, black as a foot up a bull's butt and constantly humming and flashing in their mysterious way.

Pax has his feet up on his spacious desk. If the old adage 'you can't trust a man with a clean desk' is true, my buddy is super trustworthy as his is piled six inches high, but at least in some kind of order that only he understands.

He knows it's me, as he says I'm the only one who comes in the back, takes the stairs three at a time, and comes in without paying the proper respect of an announcement. He has his face buried in some kind of manual, but glances up. "What the fuck, over?" he says, barely giving me a glance, then returning his attention to the book. He's always been able to concentrate, even with AK47 shells or RPG's singing overhead.

"I'm getting close to chasing this G5 and need a bad ass pilot."

He looks up, a little irritated at being interrupted. "I got a couple of guys, both pilots, both got there ass canned from United for being too gungho, both ex-Navy fighter jocks. It's all in the report that's piled over there on the side counter." He goes back to work dismissing me, so I take the hint and head over and pick up a three inch thick pile of printouts.

As usual, Pax has more background info than I can absorb in a week's reading. He's got more background info on Wedgeworth and his company, has put a Trojan horse into his personal computer and one into his secretary's—the beautiful Tatya—and has been recording all keystrokes on both for over twenty four hours, and is in the process of doing the same to a Paraguayan gentleman, General Hector Maldonado. But that's not the most important job he has, as I can't re-steal a very sophisticated aircraft without a skilled pilot, and hopefully co-pilot, and—almost too much to ask for—two guys with great big gonads who don't mind the occasional gun battle and probably fleeing from the Paraguayan air force...if the little country has one to be concerned with.

I have to laugh, as an inch of the book is a systems manual for a G5. I guess it's important that my guys know how to start the damn thing.

I get another belly laugh when I read about the guys Pax has turned up to serve as pilots and back up for me. Everett Alvarez is a hotshot F-18 pilot who left the Marine Corps and got qualified in multi-engine, then went on to a job with United...and was canned for screwing a flight attendant in the driver's seat while his plane was on autopilot and the co-pilot was in the head barfing up his guts with the flu.

The second guy was also a F-18 jock, and also a United forced-retiree, who was canned for being a hotshot and flying his passenger plane like it was a Navy fighter on a carrier approach.

Pax has done it again, as both the pilots he's found are hotshots, out of work, and one of them has done a short term job for Blackwater, the mercenary company who decries the title 'mercenary' and prefers being called 'paramilitary'.

And speaking of paramilitary, we'll need arms just in case things get really tough. Pax has located a couple of names for us, one in Argentina and one in Brazil, both bad boys and both located just over the border from Paraguay, both near the city of Ciudad del Este.

After buzzing through the manual, I pick up my iPhone and call Blumenthal at CalGeoCyber. To my surprise, he takes the call and doesn't do the normal Jewish make-'em-wait-twenty-minutes, I'm-more-important-than-you bullshit.

"Make it quick," he says in the way of a greeting.

"*Generalisimo* Hector Maldonado?"

"Right, No. 1 guy at the Paraguayan Air Force and a major political power in Paraguayan politics, a problem for us as he continues to push their Attorney General to sue us because his people are too stupid to operate the systems we installed for their military; Army, Navy, Marine and Air force."

"So, is he our guy?"

"That's your job, not mine. My job is contracts and defending us in case he's successful in convincing his country to continue to sue us."

"I want everything you have on him and any other contacts CalGeo has with Paraguayans. And I need it ASAP as I'm heading down there shortly."

"I'll have to check with Wedgeworth—"

"As I recall, he told you to cooperate—"

"I'll have to check."

"Check. Write this down." I give him a general email address and a drop-file name for Weatherwax Internet Service in case the file is large, which it shouldn't be, then ring off.

My next call is to Alvarez, AKA his hotshot Navy call sign, Wetback, who agrees to fly into McCarran, as does Chad Madsen, AKA his call sign, Madman. Alvarez tells me he's fluent in Spanish, so that's a plus.

And as easy as that, presuming the pilots work out, I've got a team put together.

Chapter Twelve

To my great surprise in reading deeper, one of the most interesting things to surface from the study Pax provided is the presence of Al Quaeda, Hizbollah and Hamas in what's called the triple frontier, where Paraguay, Brazil and Argentina share a common border. Twenty thousand Middle Eastern immigrants, mainly from Lebanon and Syria, provide a basis for these fears. It's reputed to be a hotbed of money laundering, arms trading, counterfeiting, and dope traffic. Arms for dope is a major element of the trafficking. Latin American terrorist groups, mainly the Revolutionary Armed Forces of Columbia and *Sendero Luminosos*, or Shining Path, operate freely across porous borders. The reports say the U.S. believes ten to twelve billion is funneled through the area each year, with Hizbollah being the primary beneficiary.

I may not be charging Wedgeworth nearly enough. Dealing with fat, complacent government bureaucrats is one thing; dealing with trained Muslim terrorists another altogether.

The good news: I should be able to buy whatever arms I need. The bad: I'll be buying from guys who'd probably love to have a—or maybe I should say another—Marine Corps hide tacked to their outhouse walls.

With luck there's still a small Marine Corps force contingency stationed in Paraguay, and with much greater luck, I'll have some kind of in with the boys there. After all, we are birds of a feather, even if mine have been slightly singed.

In 2005 the Bush administration, fearing the uprising of another Hugo Chavez in the area, cut a deal with Paraguay to build a base in *Corazon de America*, Paraguay, the heart of South America, and a Marine Corps force of some six hundred was deployed to do so. Now it's a major airport at Mariscal Estigarribia, larger than the international airport at Asuncion, the capital, with facilities rumored to be able to house sixteen thousand troops and structures which far exceed the requirements of the Paraguayan Air Force. The base stands vacant of U.S. Marines now, but can easily be put back into operation for U.S. forces should the need arise.

Cries of American expansionism and the old cries of "Yankee go home," rang throughout the three countries as well as from Columbia, Venezuela, Guyana, Peru and Bolivia, particularly when Paraguay's congress gave Marine Corps personnel diplomatic immunity from prosecution...from the base commander right down to the lowest grunt. Too bad that immunity doesn't carry over to Marines with general courts-martial!

I've got a few hours to kill before my pilots arrive at the McCarran Airport, thank God only a half hour apart, which gives me time to visit my ministorage and see what I think I can get away with taking through customs and onto an international flight. I've collected quite a bag of tricks over the years.

Most of my disguise gear—I've got a buddy who's a makeup expert in Hollywood—will pass: a wig or two, fillers to flare my cheeks and nose and change the shape of my face, a bill cap with plastic pieces that fit behind my ears and flare them like Dumbo, and a half dozen pairs of contacts to change the color of my eyes. I also pack jungle camo gear...clothes are clothes, although upon close inspection the average border guard or airport inspector might notice gear that looks paramilitary. I also pack three palm-size two-way radios. My weaponry is limited to a belt with a removable garrote wire and a pen that contains enough mace to knock down a rhino but looks innocent enough. I'd like to have my twenty four inch square quadcopter along but it's too big, too delicate, to pack; but I do take the controller and the detachable GoPro camera as I can set up the camera, and watch what it sees in real time on the controller. I rearrange the stuff in my bug-out bag, eliminating all that will arouse the ire of border guards, but do include some first aid gear, a water-pump-filter and purifying tablets, and a jungle survival manual. And even though I hope to have two Spanish speaking partners, I throw in an English-Spanish dictionary. I can find the *banos* and order in the *restorante*, but that's about the extent of my *Español*.

When one's going on a job to recover a G5 one plans to leave the country in high style, but one never knows when he might be, instead, slogging through a jungle fighting leeches, snakes and jaguars...and—worse but more likely—dysentery and malaria-carrying mosquitos.

As I'm travelling as a businessman, I take one respectable looking carry on and a matching bag which I'll check, and go through the few decent rags that change me from bodyguard grunt to blue blazer, slacks, and loafer clad respectable traveler. I have a half dozen driver's licenses in a variety of names, but only one passport, so I'm going under my real name, Mike Reardon. I sort through my credit cards and business cards to make sure I don't have anything in my possession that will raise red flags. Using a fake passport from a sophisticated country is a real risk now that Interpol's stolen travel document registry is active. A keystroke and you may be discovered as a phony.

I finish in time to settle down and make a couple of phone calls.

The first is to Carmen, my travel mate. I give her my passport number and tell her we plan to leave for Paraguay in two days so she'll need to use her influence to get that travel visa for me. Then I call an old girlfriend, Jennifer, who I had more than a passing interest in, but who seemed to tire of the fact I would disappear for weeks without calling.

Women seldom understand that when dope dealers and pimps, and many times police, are trying to beat you to death or fill you full of lead, you forget the niceties of relationships. She seems happy to get my call and agrees to lunch, but has to go to work shortly thereafter—she's a keno runner at one of the local clubs—so there goes any chance for more than a hug to recall old times. Ka ka happens.

It's just as well, as late this afternoon I have to meet up with my potential pilots. And as I recall, wham bam thank you ma'am wasn't her style anyway.

I just have time to visit the local Barnes and Noble and pick up a couple of text-type books on Avionics, as my cover is as a salesperson for Paragon Avionics, an actual company, that's headquartered in Philadelphia. I met a guy who was an engineer for them. Pax has the guy's card and his in-house graphics person is making me a couple of dozen replicas, only with the name Mike Reardon and the title Director of Sales. I have a collection of cards, as you never know when you might want to be a Drug Enforcement Agent or an accountant or a lingerie salesman, and with today's scanners and printers, it's easy to do. Total BS, but unless someone in Paraguay invests in a long distance call to the company, I'm home free.

You can be anyone you want to be, so long as you keep your mouth shut and your primary response is "I'll check into it." All you need is the basics of any skill or industry.

I'm a little maudlin during my lunch with the beautiful Jennifer, and not surprised to learn that she's tied up with a pit boss. I wonder how serious it is as she's having lunch with me and gives me a lingering hug and nibble on the neck when we part. Still, I'm sure she's a long way from being willing to put up with a will-o-the-wisp who comes and goes, a guy she'd only pass like ships in the night. So much for long term relationships, that's one thing even the repairman can't seem to keep repaired. Again, ka ka happens.

It's time to pick up my pilots and see if I can make a deal, and if they're tough enough to get involved and willing to take a big risk for a big return.

Chapter Thirteen

Everete Alvarez is the first to touch down. I'm waiting near the luggage carousel, where we'd agreed to meet, for his flight from San Diego, with his picture in hand, when he approaches. I probably would have spotted him anyway. Navy jet jocks have an I'm-hot-shit-don't-fuck-with-me swagger about them that's hard to miss. He's a medium height guy, but with shoulders like some granite mountains I've seen, and a barrel chest that looks like he could hold enough air to stay underwater for a week. His hair is black, straight, and Elvis-long but perfectly combed, and he's got a bushy mustache, perfectly trimmed, that would shame Pancho Villa. And he's a clothes hog, obvious by the sharp ceases, color coordination, and military shine on the shoes.

He sticks out a hand when I walk up to where he stops to wait for his luggage.

"You got checked luggage?" I ask.

"Affirmative," he says, and nods as he shakes.

"Pretty sure you were getting the job?" I ask, with a hint of a dig.

"Fucking-A," he says, then adds, "...but if it doesn't work out, I'm in Vegas, so what the hell."

I laugh. "Let's get your bag then put it down over on one of those benches and wait for Madsen. He's due in a half hour."

"Madman Madsen?"

"One and the same."

"Good, he's a good man. A crazy fuck, but a good man to have at your back."

The luggage starts dumping off, and his bag is the third one, so we head to a bench.

"What's the gig?" he asks as he parks it.

"As you were told on the phone by my buddy, Weatherwax, it's a G5 that's gone missing. All you guys have to do is fly it out, presuming we can get you in the cockpit."

"Out of?"

"Paraguay."

"So, who stole her?"

I have to smile. "If it proves to be who it appears to be, the stud duck of the Paraguayan Air Force."

Now it's his turn to laugh, but it's a low one. Then he asks, "So, we're stealing it back, flying it out of a country with...I presume...with some fighters of some sort, and we're gonna do so without getting shot to shit?"

"That's about it. You got the nads for it?"

"My nads grow with the pay. What's it pay?"

"A grand a week guarantee, win or lose, and your expenses. We get home with the goods, and you get a quarter mil."

"And what's your take?" he asks, eying me suspiciously.

"Enough to pay you and Madsen a quarter mil each, if I get back here with the goods."

"When?"

"I'm going down day after tomorrow and when I know what's up, I'll call. I presume your passport is in order?"

"You bet. How about a visa?"

"That'll be handled. I've got an in at their embassy."

"So, if we end up in some deep dark prison in the middle of South America, does the grand a week continue?"

"Hard to say and harder to pay, as I'll be in the cell next to you. I'll give you half of every rat I catch…how's that?"

He smiles, a little sardonically, "About what I expected."

"So, you in?"

"Balls to the wall. No guts, no air medals," he says, and extends a hand and we shake. "So," he asks, "you want me to hang here until you call?"

"Pax has room to put you and Madsen up for a few days. Unless you need to get back to the wife and kids?"

"No kids, and the ex-wife is too damn good a shot to get close to."

Again, I laugh. We BS about the service until I glance at my watch and see it's time for Madsen to arrive. I move on down to the luggage carousel that's receiving baggage from the flight from Miami, and don't have to wait long.

Chad Madsen is my height, thin, looking like a runner, with a sharp nose and penetrating green eyes. But like Alvarez, he's got a handshake that would crush a billiard ball. And he, like Alvarez, is cocksure and full of piss and vinegar.

"What's the job?" he asks right off. "We gonna steal a MIG from Moscow, or what?"

These guys are gonna be a hoot to work with. "No, no Moscow. Just a nice little ride that I hope we're taking out of South America."

"Little ride? That can't be worth my time."

"Little G5 ride."

"That's more like it. You flying the right seat?"

"Nope. I'm a passenger, I hope. But you know the guy who is. You remember Everete Alvarez?"

"Wetback. Damn right I remember him. We were on the Independence together."

"He's over against the wall. Let's go get him, then go get a beer."

"Or six," he says. He heads over to Alvarez and has a hand out before I can catch up.

By the time Pax is ready to close the office, Wetback, Madman and I have told enough war stories to fill a small library and downed enough beer to float the *Independence*. I'm liking these guys a lot, and my team is set.

I call Carmen with their passport numbers and info on the flight Pax's girl has got us set up to travel on. It's a little over seventeen hundred bucks, round trip, open return date—which I hope I won't need—with a stopover in Panama. Twelve hours flying time.

She gives me a small piece of information that plasters a smile on my face that you couldn't blow off with C4, even though it's going to cost me a cool five grand, under the table to a friend of hers in the Paraguayan embassy. I'll be travelling with a 'diplomatic exclusion. Which means I can get aboard without being searched. I'd love to strap my sniper rifle on my back, but that would be a little obvious...so it'll have to be confined to a couple of handguns.

I should be able to get a real schooling on Paraguay during the long flight, and should be a lot more prepared when I arrive, thanks to the reading I'll be doing, to Carmen, and to the diplomatic exclusion stamp on my visa and passport.

Chapter Fourteen

It's barely light when we board the first leg to Panama City. We arrive there at three PM then leave for Asuncion after a short layover, arriving at Paraguay's capital just before midnight. It's hard to figure looking at a map, but Paraguay, in the center of South America, is five hours earlier than Los Angeles, two earlier than New York. Midnight there is only seven PM L.A. time, so the flight's not quite so bad as it seems. Carmen's arranged to have family pick us up and deliver me to my hotel, La Mision, a converted old mansion with a newer five storey annex. She's staying with an aunt and uncle.

Copa is the national airlines of Panama. Pax is happy with it and tells me it received some award for the best Central-South American airline, and believe me, what experience I've had they cover the spectrum from awful to exquisite. Brazil, Argentina, Chile and Peru have flights and service to rival any in the world. From Copa's location in the Tom Bradley International Terminal to their service I'd rank them right up there, of course, when you're flying first class you expect the best.

I relax when I find we're travelling in a 737, and one that appears to have great maintenance, at least from what I see on the interior. And the Latina who's working the first class section is a major wow...if their mechanical maintenance is half has good as her personal maintenance has been, we're fine.

Carmen and I are seated side by side in seats almost fully reclining, and each has a screen for movies, TV and games. She's wisely dressed in a velour suit, soft slipper loafers, with her hair tied back. This isn't her first rodeo.

It's good it's early as I want to grill her for a few hours, and do, all the way to Panama City. I'm pleased to learn that her father is an admiral in the Paraguayan Navy, and she has an uncle in the lower house of Parliament—the Chamber of Deputies—like our Congressmen. Her cousin is a helicopter pilot in the Air Force, and I silently thank God he's not the pilot of one of their two attack choppers. Paraguay has almost three dozen surface ships—old, but serviceable—due to their access to the Atlantic via the Paraguay-Parana Rivers, with their main base being in Asuncion. Most are river patrol boats, not qualifying as ships.

Carmen is like an encyclopedia on her country. Pax couldn't have done better by me.

She finally gives up after we've been fed an excellent supper, and sleeps. I'm too keyed up, going into a situation that could make me over a million bucks after all my expenses, or could cost me my freedom.

I'm pretty sure the powers that be in Paraguay won't much give a damn that the airplane I plan to steal, is, in fact, a stolen airplane. Brought to mind is an old buddy of mine who often said, "I don't much give a damn if you steal something I bought, just don't steal something I stole." Seems he thought stealing something took more effort than buying something.

And even though the Paraguayans filched the airplane, if they in fact did, they think they're justified in doing so, as CalGeoCyber didn't do their job. Or so it's believed.

I'm not here to judge. I'm not being paid to judge, I'm only paid if and when I return the airplane.

My hotel is as classy as it appears on the web, and a bottle of fine Chilean *vino rojo* is awaiting in the middle of a basket of fruit, some of it, the likes of which I've never seen. I hope I'll have some time to get a taste of the country and the local eats, but if I could find the airplane tomorrow, then call my guys and get them here and get the hell out of Dodge with the goods, I'd do that in a heartbeat.

When I was dropped off by Carmen's uncle, Manolo Juarez, a stately gray haired gentleman with a military bearing but a little short on English, her last words were "don't call me before noon." Which is fine with me as I plan to visit the American embassy before my search for the G5. Manolo, she's told me, is her father's brother, so I presume Carmen's been married before as her name is Diaz. The subject never came up as we were too busy talking business.

It's almost two AM when I get in my room, but I'm still awake with the sun, and am soon showered, shaved, dressed in an open collar and coat, but a light one, as it's February in South America. The seasons are opposite so it's the dead of Summer, only slightly cooler than January, a little over thirty degrees centigrade average, which is over ninety degrees Fahrenheit. You'd think that the country was high altitude, with the Andes not far away, but it only varies from a little over sea level to a little under three thousand feet elevation. So the elevation doesn't cool things off much. As a result of great fertile plains with an excellent shallow aquifer, Paraguay is the fourth largest producer of soybeans in the world, and a great agricultural cornucopia of other crops.

Some of this I've learned from Carmen, some I've read.

I doubt if the rest of the country eats like I was served for breakfast: *cafe con leche*, coffee with milk; *cocido con leche*, yerba tea with milk. *Chipa*, a kind of cheesy bread made from yuca flour; some guava jam with that. Toast, butter, cheese and jam. And *medialunas*, croissants, with yogurt and fresh fruit. I was offered *bife*, battered beef steak called milanesá, and *empanadas*, wonderful pastries of flaky crust full of meat, but I was too full.

On going to the desk to change some American dollars for Paraguayan guarani, I'm pleased to find I have a handful of bills in my pocket with 100,000.00 printed on them. However, since the exchange rate is 4,500 guarani to the buck, making the bills worth about twenty-two bucks, I guess it's not too impressive.

Sipping my last coffee refill, I am surprised by a gentleman in a frumpy tan seersucker suit who crosses the small dining room, extends a hand, and asks, "Mr. Reardon?"

I rise, actually a little shocked to be called by name, but I take the hand and shake, if you could call the fishy-floppy hand shakable. His hair is thin and a little wild, were it thicker he'd be an Albert Einstein look-alike. The suit is wrinkled, his tie spotted with his breakfast or last night's supper, but he has a handsome straw hat in hand, maybe an expensive Panama and it makes me jealous I wasn't in Panama City long enough to buy one. I say nothing until he asks, "May I join you?"

"Sure, why not. You know my name. Are you with the hotel?"

He sits and waves the waitress over. "Tea, milk, sugar," he asks, in English. And she hurries away.

"And you are?" I ask.

"Theo Gann, I'm the Assistant Director for International Development at the American embassy here."

"Aw, you're here to help me peddle some avionics? I was going to drop over to the embassy this morning to make a social call and see if I could enlist your help. Are you willing to help?"

"No, probably not. I know exactly who you are and we're wondering why you're here. You understand that bounty hunters have no legality anywhere outside the U.S.A.?"

"Of course. I'm not here hunting a failure-to-appear. I actually do very little of that."

He eyes me carefully, then asks, "So, why are you here?"

I have to think fast. I am not prepared to be challenged by my own embassy. "Actually, I'm a tourist."

"I doubt that," he says, again studying me through watery gray eyes.

"You may doubt it if you'd like, but I'm down here with my girlfriend who's a Paraguayan citizen."

"You arrived with Carmen Diaz, a former employee of the Paraguayan Consulate in Los Angeles. You're saying she's your girlfriend?"

"Fiancée, actually, but she doesn't want her family to know that until I've had a chance to work my way into their hearts." I'm proud of myself, thinking fast.

"You'll pardon me," he says, "but I think that's total bullshit."

"Me too. I never thought she'd consider a guy like me."

He laughs, then coughs, then says, "I don't mean that, I mean I doubt the veracity of that explanation of why you're in Paraguay."

"Your privilege. And I presume you're actually CIA?"

"No. International Development. However, you arrived with a diplomatic exclusion stamp on your passport, allowing you to pass through Homeland Security in the states and through customs here. That makes no sense to us as you're a private citizen...an American. It's not like you're a diplomatic official or federal officer. Our people worked all night putting together a dossier on you."

"Again, your privilege. My girlfriend doesn't like the hassle." I'm quiet a few seconds while we eye each other, then continue, "So, they're no longer calling you CIA guys cultural attaché...now it's International Development?"

He ignores the question. "So, did you bring anything into the country that might be against Paraguayan law?"

"I would never do such a thing," I lie, while the waitress places his tea and milk on the table.

"You know your embassy does not protect you if you break a host country's laws."

"Jeeze," I say, taking a page out of Wedgeworth's book, "I hope I don't have a traffic accident or something."

"You are a total bullshitter, Reardon. I have a half-inch thick file on you. Let's not be causing an international incident. We might just join in your prosecution, should you embarrass us here in Paraguay."

That makes me chuckle. "Mr. Gann, the State Department has long been capable of embarrassing themselves...they need no help from some poor old boy who's merely trying to make points with his future in-laws. I'd think after Benghazi you guys would keep your mouths shut—of course that was State, not CIA—so maybe your guys weren't at fault."

He takes one sip of his tea, then stands, adjusts, then tips his hat, rearranges his sagging pants under a little pot belly, and walks away. I have to smile. It's not like a CIA guy to wear a belt and suspenders. He's a real cautious type.

I can't help myself, and call after him, "Don't worry about the check, I'll get it." He glances back and I get the feeling he'd love to give me the finger, but he pushes through the door and I can feel the rush of heat from outside all the way across the room.

Why didn't I pick July, when it's winter in Paraguay?

Chapter Fifteen

I talk to the desk and get them to call me a taxi with a driver who speaks good English and can double as a guide, then make a deal with Alex Benitez. He must know all the good restaurants as he can barely fit under the wheel, but he's got a great smile, even with one missing eye tooth, and is fluent in the King's English.

It's nine AM when I climb in his cab—the South American version of a Ford—and we agree that he'll drive me anywhere up until noon for forty bucks, as long as we end up back at the hotel. Too bad I'm not heading half way across the country, but all I want is to familiarize myself with the city.

Asuncion is the capital of Paraguay, is on the west border with Argentina across Rio Paraguay. She's a city of a half million in a country of five million, and like most Central and South American cities, she's diverse. Alex tries to avoid the slums, but I insist on making a comprehensive round and a complete circle of one particular point of interest, the Silvio Pettirossi International Airport, which is located in Luque, a suburb. It was formerly Presidente Stroessner International Airport, but since the *presidente*, read dictator, fell out of favor and was overthrown, it was renamed for a famous Paraguayan aviator.

I ask Alex to pull up near an eight foot cyclone fence where I can see a quarter mile across the tarmac to a cluster of buildings and aircraft. It's a good thing I brought my Nikon binocs. I'm no expert, but I recognize a 707, the country's flag painted on her tail, which Alex informs me is their Air Force One. Later at the hotel, studying some pics I've taken with my iPhone, I go online and identify two old but seemingly well maintained C-47's, circa WWII; two C212 Aviocars, high wing turboprop transports that are no threat; a WFU CV240 transport with Air Force markings which, like the C-47's, should be in a museum somewhere; and several AT33A's, pure jets that were originally American Navy or Air Force trainers. These appear to have some sort of light machine guns mounted under the wings so they're a threat with a top speed of around four hundred knots. The good news, the G5 will leave them in the dust, or clouds in this instance.

Three Embraer Xavantes and three EMB 312 Tucanos are also good aircraft, probably hand-me-downs from Brazil, but they also can't keep up with Mr. Grumman's jewel. So unless there's something in the air, at another base, or in the Paraguayan Navy or Marine fleet that I don't know about, once we're in the air we're home free.

That's the good news. The bad is I don't see a G5 parked anywhere, though there are three hangars, any of which is large enough to house the target. One of them has a guard posted outside.

I email this info to Pax to pass along to Madman and Wetback; then it's time to call Carmen.

"I'm up, dressed, and ready for brunch," she says before I have a chance to ask.

"I have a cab and good driver waiting outside, if that's helpful."

"It is. I don't want to borrow my aunt or uncle's car...besides, he's at work. Let's see, rather than you coming all the way over here, how about I meet you at the Catedral Metropolitana de Asuncion...the Cathedral. Your driver will know. There's a beautiful park across from it and lots of vendors stands."

"So, we're having lunch from the vendor's stands?"

"Ha! We're having lunch in the best restaurant in Asuncion, of course. Bolsi is not far from our meeting place, and you must try the surubi."

"Of course we are eating at the best place in town. You buying?"

She giggles. "*Señor*, it's the best *restorante* in Paraguay. You're in South America, where women are still women and men, thank God, are still men...and the men, who are real men, treat the ladies like ladies."

"Okay, I'm properly chastised."

"Meet you on the front steps. You should see the beautiful old church. Say forty minutes?"

"That's ten to one. I'll be there."

Alex is more than happy to finish the day out with me, for another forty bucks, and I'm pleased to have him do so, as he not only knows every major building in the city, but seems to know a little about her underbelly...like most urban cab drivers.

On the way to meet Carmen, he tells me about the rougher neighborhoods in the city, known there as barrios just as they are in Los Angeles and other southwestern cities. We're headed to one known as Cetedral, named because of the location of the Cathedral, but there's also La Encarnacion, General Diaz, San Roque, and La Charcarita, and he assures me I can find almost anything I want there. I don't mention I'd like to find a couple of RPG's and three or four AK47's or AR15's.

I'll probably have to head to the Tri-Border region for those toys, if I need them at all, but that's putting the cart before the proverbial horse. First I have to locate the target.

As she promised, she's waiting on the steps. I exit the cab, ask him to wait, and join her.

"Can we walk to the restaurant?" I ask.

"Only a few blocks, and I need the exercise."

I return to Alex and ask him to pick us up at Bolsi in an hour and a half. He salutes, and heads out to get his own lunch.

The cathedral is beautiful, like a dozen others I've seen, but I ooh and ahh and show Carmen how appreciative I am of her country. Then we head out for a brisk walk to lunch. Bolsi is in an old building on the corner of Estrella and Alberdi, with a dining area and bar up front, but she leads me to the back. For a second I fear she's headed for a patio, as I'm already sweated through, but she doesn't. Alex is already there, parked outside, windows down, taking a siesta.

Carmen never ceases to surprise me, and the maître d' runs over and embraces her with a hug and kiss on both cheeks. We're seated at the best table in the house, under the air conditioning, and she orders for both of us in Spanish so rapidly I don't get a word of it.

Surubi turns out to be a catfish from the local river, which grows as large as a man, and the helping I get would be a roast in most other places. And it's delicious. We each down two large local beers, have dessert and coffee—and I am sweating the check, which turns out to be a lousy thirty bucks each, plus the tip. I'm starting to like Paraguay. To bad; with luck and a successful mission, they'll soon dislike me.

"So," she asks, as we finish our coffee, "you like Bolsi?"

"I like Bolsi. I like you. I like Paraguay. But I have to get to work. I need to get on the airport."

"Can't you use your new job as a Avionics salesman?" she asks, and eyes me a little coyly. She has yet to know my real mission, only that I'm retrieving something stolen. And I don't want her to know. The less she knows, the more deniability she has.

"I can, I guess. But didn't you say you have a relative in the Air Force?"

"Retired. But my cousin is still active. You're having supper at my uncles tonight, if that's okay with you?"

"Perfect." I guess it's time to fess up. "By the way, some dickwad—"

"Dick wad?" she asks.

"Sorry, some guy from the American embassy jumped me at the hotel this morning and caught me a little unprepared, asking why I was in Paraguay."

"And?"

"And, I told him you were my fiancée and I was here to meet your family."

She laughs, to my great relief, then bites a lip and looks at me, then laughs again and asks, "So, where's my diamond?"

"It's on order, *querida*." I know enough Spanish to say sweetheart.

"Right, *carino*," she answers. "I'll hold my breath for that one."

"Besides, you're making enough to buy your own diamond."

"What kind of fiancée are you?" She laughs again, then adds, "Let's get out of here. I have to go to the *carniceria* for *mi tia*."

"Oh, God, I couldn't eat another bite."

"You'll be able to by supper time...that's ten here in Paraguay."

"Right, I forgot."

"Go back to the room and get a nap. They'll think you're a Latino, taking your *siesta*."

Then I have an important thought. "Will your cousin, the helo pilot, be there."

"He's invited, along with his wife and six *muchachos*."

"Great. Can I give you some money for the market?"

She gives me a disgusted look. "Don't start out insulting my aunt."

"Yes, ma'am. Can I have Alex drop you?"

"No, you're going the other way. Get some rest. You'll need it to stand up to your new in-laws." She's still laughing as I excuse myself.

Chapter Sixteen

I don't head for the hotel, but rather back to the airport. It's not me who gets a siesta, but Alex, who's more than willing to park where I have a view of the tarmac and hangars large enough to house the G5 and sleep while I keep an eye out, hoping the doors will open and I can see the contents. One finally does, and I see it's full of helicopters—two old Huey's from the Vietnam era, one French, a nice unit, an Alouette, I believe, and a couple of old Hughes models. Unarmed, other than the Hueys, and no threat to a fast moving G5, I'd guess.

But the guards patrolling the tarmac and the hangars are another matter. It's hard to tell at this distance, but they appear to have sidearms and are carrying Hechler and Koch's HK416's, a formidable weapon. And there are at least eight guards. There are two light vehicles, with 50 cals mounted on elevated pods and two guards inside, and they are constantly patrolling. Others are moving on foot in what seems to be a predetermined pattern. Only one hangar seems to have a pair of permanent guards posted on either side of the hangar doors.

Just as I'm about to awaken Alex to head back to the hotel, a hangar door rolls aside enough to allow a small service truck to enter, and I get a glance at a winglet, the turned up wingtip of a G5. This wing is dark blue, and the Wedgeworth plane was white, but a paint job solves that in a few heartbeats. I have lots of identifying serial numbers in my file from various airplane components, so to be absolutely sure, I have to get inside that hangar and spend some time digging around so I can be absolutely right I have the right aircraft. Stealing the wrong airplane would not only be embarrassing, but probably incarcerating, and that would be bad fun in a Paraguayan *jusgados*.

Of course it would be the hangar with the permanent guards posted outside.

We get back to the hotel in time for me to catch a cat nap, dress in casual attire, and head down to the hotel bar. I'm due at the Juarez residence at eight p.m. and have asked Alex to show up in time to get there promptly. There's both a flower vendor and a shop stocking wine across from the hotel, so I wander over and pick up a bunch for my hostess and find a bottle of what I'm assured is a great red. I'm not used to paying six bucks for the best bottle of wine in the house.

There are only six stools at the hotel bar, and the manager is there taking inventory and speaks excellent English, so I order a Jack neat and strike up a conversation with him while he works. Sancho Alfonso, graying at the temples, with coke bottle thick eyeglasses, is friendly enough, in a businesslike way.

"So, Señor Alfonso, you have been in hospitality a long time?"

"For many years."

"Always here in Asuncion?"

"No, I worked in Miami for a half dozen years."

"You must get many North Americans here?"

He gives me a smile. "And you must travel in Central and South America a great deal, if you're sympathetic to not presuming the term American applies only to those from the U.S.

"Some. I'm a sales rep for an avionics company."

"So, you are here meeting with our government or military."

"I hope to."

"We had a gentleman here at the hotel for a week who was hired to fly the new government aircraft."

That perks up my ears. "Oh, I may know him."

"Señor Glascock?"

"I believe I have met him. Was he travelling with another gentleman?" So, Glascock is in with the den of thieves. I'm wondering if Toby Bartlett, the Wedgeworth co-pilot, is one of the bad guys as well.

"No, he was alone."

I yawn, as if I'm just mildly interested, then ask, "I'd like to say hello to him. You know where he can be reached?"

"No, he checked out without a forwarding address, but the military would know as he never required a cab. He was picked up by an Air Force vehicle."

"I think his partner was named…" I act as if I'm thinking. "Barnett or Bartlett?"

"No, he was alone."

I ask for my check and he says don't worry, he'll add it to my bill and I kill the Jack, leave a buck tip on the bar, and wander out front to wait for Alex and make a couple of calls. I still have forty five minutes to kill. My first call is to Pax, to inform him that I'm on the right track, to get the pilots scheduled to leave, and to get him to run down my old buddy Skip Allen, also Marine Recon. who served with the two of us and has helped me with recoveries several times. Then I ask him about his research into Henry 'Hank' Hausman. He seems impressed with the guy, so my next call is to Hank on the throwaway phone I left with him.

"You're a man of your word," he says, not bothering with hello. I guess he hasn't given the number to anyone else.

"I am, here's the deal...." I explain the job to him, and the pay, and give him Pax's number. I'll have five guys total, very competent guys, with Hank, Skip and the two pilots on their way in two days, if I don't find reason to call them off.

I really liked Penny Bartlett, Toby Bartlett's wife, whom I met in Goleta and interviewed. I'm now in great fear that Toby Bartlett was an unwilling participant in the filching of the G5, and if so, was not allowed to live, much less return home. It's amazing what fifty million dollars worth of aircraft might motivate someone to do. And I'm afraid Toby's been done.

He's been missing for a very long time, but to make sure he's not safely at home, I call Penny. She should be getting off work about now; seven thirty PM Asuncion time is two thirty PM Goleta time, and I imagine her class gets out of school by three. She answers.

"Mrs. Bartlett."

"Yes."

"Mike Reardon...you remember me."

"Yes. Do you have news about Toby?" she asks quickly, and I don't have to ask, so I make it nothing more than a concern call.

"No, ma'am. I just wanted to check in with you and make sure you were getting on okay."

"Are you in the area?"

"Nope. In fact I'm out of the country. I'll call again to check on you when I return."

"That's sweet of you. Are you on the track of the plane?"

"I'm still working on it. I'll call if I turn anything up."

"Thanks. Thanks so very much."

So, Toby Bartlett is among the missing. It doesn't bode well for the Bartletts.

Chapter Seventeen

Alex said it would take twenty minutes to get to the Juarez *rancho*, or *estancia*, and he's right on time to pick me up.

As we move through the suburbs, I see more and more of the agricultural aspect of the country—some tall sugar cane fields in the distance and as we near our destination, coffee bushes standing ten feet tall and bursting with red berries.

It's just a short distant north of town to the Juarez *estancia* and a stone gate, with a gatekeeper, who waves us through when Alex reports the name of his passenger. It's a half-mile of winding lane through ten-foot-tall coffee bushes to a stately old rambling one storey house on a low bluff overlooking Rio Paraguay, a quarter mile distant. The gatekeeper must have called ahead as Carmen is waiting at a stone walkway when I'm dropped off. She instructs Alex to return at midnight, hooks an arm through mine, and leads me up a lane rimmed with brilliant blooms that could only grow so lush in a semi-tropical climate. We arrive at an impressive five-foot-wide plank door with a pair of full size Andean flamingo carvings therein. The ten pound brass knocker is the head of a flamingo.

A half dozen folks, and two German shorthairs, are lined up to receive their American guest. Carmen leads me down the line and introduces me to her aunt, Josefa, who gleams as I hand her the large bouquet of flowers, then I shake with her Uncle Manolo and hand him the bottle of wine. He eyes it and I get the feeling he's about to shrug, but he's too polite.

I've found all Paraguayans to be polite and quiet spoken, and I'm beginning to wish I was not about to alienate more than half the country.

Carmen's cousin, whom I'm most interested to meet, is a helo pilot and I hope he's stationed at the hangars I visited earlier in the day. I'll discover that later. Micha Santos, like his uncle, has an upright military bearing and I get the impression all pilots are alike. He snaps his heels together when we shake and emanates self-confidence and the cockiness that goes along with the profession. His wife, Luisa, was once a beautiful woman, but has now the inner beauty of a woman proud of the fact that she's borne six children. She has a beautiful smile, and she, too, has little English. It seems most of my conversation, other than with Carmen, will be with her cousin Micha, which pleases me until he begins grilling me about the latest in avionics. It's a good thing I've studied the sales material from Paragon Avionics, as well as a couple of light texts on the subject and some articles Pax pulled from the web on the latest advancements, as the card we've forged declares I'm a vice-president.

I did read up on collusion avoidance equipment, and manage to bullshit with the best of them on that subject. I throw out terms like TCAS, traffic alert, and collusion avoidance systems; NAVSTAR, and the accuracy of the systems so now even land surveys can be accomplished via aviation; and Chelton Flight Logic, systems that can 'see' through the clouds and other adverse weather conditions to give the pilot a visual of the surface below. But I'm quickly running out of acronyms.

Even with all that bull, he has me stumped by about the second question, and eyeballs me with more than a little curiosity when most of my answers are "I'll look into that and get back to you."

Supper, proceeded by a long grace said by our host, is a long, slow six-course affair with beef, fish they call golden dorado, and some wild bird they refer to as perdiz which is a variety of partridge, and delicious. Enough food is being run from kitchen to table to feed a small country, and I'm totally stuffed by the time the men retire to a billiard room—one wall lined with fine sporting rifles and shotguns, one with pictures of Manolo and lots of what appear to be celebrities and politicians—to partake of a few snifters of fine cognac.

I finally get around to asking, "I'd love to see your equipment...your aircraft...if that's permissible?"

In typical form, he puffs his chest out and again snaps his heels together. "When?" he asks.

"As soon as possible. I have to go on to Sao Paulo from here."

He scoffs. "The Brazilians...we outfly them in every joint operation. The Argentines are some better, but the Brazilians are too many Cariocas, playboys from Rio, who want to do nothing but play, and Paulistas, from Sao Paulo, who are too anal and uptight to fly well...and all of them in the Brazilian Air Force. Their minds...the Cariocas...are on women, not aviation. And the Paulistas only care about how well their aircraft are shined and maintained."

I laugh and click glasses with him.

"Would ten AM be too early for you, Miguel?" he asks, calling me by the Spanish inclination of my name.

"No, Micha, that would be perfect."

"I'll have a car pick you up."

"That's too kind. I can take a cab."

"No, I insist. My *comandante*, Colonel Vargas, will be pleased to have you visit. We are very proud of our Air Force, and very interested in new developments in avionics."

"Ten, then." Again, we clink glasses. "Your Colonel's first name?"

"Emilio, but he's a very formal man. So, please, wear a tie, and never be so familiar as to call him anything other than Colonel, or Colonel Vasquez."

I nod, but I want to know who I'm dealing with, and a first name is necessary.

So, I'm in, at least as far as the helo hangar. With luck, they're proud of showing off their whole stable of aircraft, particularly their new G5.

When it's time to take my leave, Carmen walks me out, and I inform her that I won't be needing her tomorrow, at least not in the morning.

As soon as I get a good signal, I call Pax and ask him to email me info on Colonel Emilio Vargas before ten AM Paraguay time tomorrow.

I have a full dossier on Colonel Emilio Vargas and have read it by the time I'm waiting on the step for the arrival of the Air Force driver and car.

Upon reading the Colonel's background, I get the feeling that things have been going far too well and that the other shoe's about to drop. Vargas attended USC twenty five years ago, was thrown off the soccer team in his junior year after being accused of rape, but exonerated after his father hired L.A.'s best, then thrown out altogether from graduate school after being arrested for drunk driving and vehicular manslaughter—a crime many thought was murder as he knew the two young men he ran down in a parking lot. He never appeared in court and disappeared from the country, not to be seen again north of the equator. When he later showed up in Paraguay, the government refused to extradite him, as his father was a Minister of Agriculture, very high up in the government of the former dictator, Stroessner. When Stroessner was deposed in 1989 the Americans seemed to have lost interest. Vargas was no longer pursued, not that the new government would have given up one of their own.

And his reputation in Paraguay has been little better. He's a bad, bad boy. I'm wondering if it's Vargas, not General Maldonado who engineered the theft of the G5.

And if so, Vargas seems the type who wouldn't worry if a young American, Toby Bartlett, disappeared in a Paraguayan swamp.

My driver, uniformed in the dress of the Paraguayan Air Force, speaks no English, so I learn nothing on the ride to the airport. There's a modern glass, steel, and concrete block building somewhat apart from the hangars. I'm delivered there, escorted inside by the driver, and motioned to take a seat in a waiting room. An attractive, uniformed young lady hurries away and reappears with Micha Santos at her side.

He's snappy as ever, and leads me back outside with, "I will give you the tour which will take a couple of hours, then we will join Colonel Vargas for lunch in his private dining room."

We take our time, starting with the 707 that's their Air Force One—a beautifully detailed and maintained aircraft, if old. We visit other aircraft on the tarmac, then he takes me into his bailiwick, the helicopter hangar. I linger over the avionics of every aircraft, eyeing each piece of equipment as if I know what the hell I'm talking about. I finally realize we're skipping the hangar housing what I perceived to be a G5, and inquire.

"That's Colonel Vargas's private hangar. He has personal items there, and shares it with General Maldonado."

"Aircraft?" I ask.

"Yes, it houses a fairly new G500, an Icon A5 capable of water take-off and landing, and a Citabria. It's a toy garage."

I know enough about my target to know the military version was called a G500. "A G500 is hardly a toy. Did they acquire it from the American military?"

"No. It was via some kind of legal settlement from an American company."

"Then probably better called a G5?" He doesn't respond. "Nice settlement. Good avionics, or can I do something for the colonel?"

"It has the very best."

"I'd love to see the Icon. I understand it's a fabulous little airplane and I've never had the chance to walk one. He must have purchased one of the very first off the production line. I've flown many a Citabria when I did some stunt flying. Tail draggers are fun."

He glances at his watch. "Maybe after lunch. Colonel Vargas doesn't tolerate tardiness. I didn't know you were a pilot, but I imagine it goes with the job?"

"Certainly. And a jumper, a parachutist, with over fifty to my credit." That part is true, although I'm hardly a pilot, only having had a few lessons.

He laughs as he strides out back toward the office building. "Out of a perfectly good aircraft. I've made two jumps, required, but I hope that is it for me."

112

By the time we get there I'd like to hang whoever invented men's neckwear, as the tie is choking me to death and my shirt is sweated through at the pits.

Thank God, the Colonel's private dining room is air conditioned, but that's not the most pleasurable part of the lunch—Vargas enters with good old Charlie Glascock close behind.

Chapter Eighteen

Isn't it great when something you want falls in your hand?

I have a picture of Glascock, but it doesn't show the red splotches on his nose and cheeks, indicating guy who spends way too much time in a bottle, nor the sagging jowls showing he's aging before his time—I figure him in his early fifties. Nor does it show the paunch hanging over his belt. This is not a guy I'd like to have flying me around the twenty two thousand feet plus Andes.

Micha introduces us. Glascock is dismissive, and even before Micha goes on to the Colonel, says, "Our equipment is all top notch, so you're wasting your time here."

I shrug, then turn to the Colonel, who shakes politely but with little enthusiasm, and gives me a look like I might be carrying Ebola or some other dreaded disease. So much for my welcome to Paraguay.

We sit around a table large enough for eight, and I'm happy to note there's a large bouquet of jungle flowers in the center of the table, so I have to lean to the side to talk to Glascock, which is just fine as the last thing I want to do is get into an avionics discussion with him. He's an asshole, but no one said he's a stupid asshole.

I'm a little surprised when Micha translates for Colonel Vargas; as after all, he did attend USC a little over twenty years ago. I get the impression he doesn't want anyone to know how well he speaks English, so I'll be very careful about what I say around him. I think he speaks it at least as well as Micha.

I do get around to asking him, "So, I understand you have an Icon? I love the little plane, at least by its advertisements and stats. I'd love to see it and give it a walk around."

He doesn't wait for Micha, but answers. "Aw, *el* Icon. You like?"

"I'd love to see it, Colonel Vargas, if you'd allow it?" My most admiring tone.

"Okay," he says, turning to Micha. "No touch. Jus' look."

"Yes, sir," Micha snaps.

We make small talk and enjoy a great lunch of cold cuts and fruit, then the Colonel is called away by the same young lady whos served us. I do recognize the word *telefono*. He shakes as if he's not going to return.

Which gives me the opportunity to slide over enough so I can see Glascock. As we enjoy a delicious cup of strong coffee, I finally get around to asking the question that's been niggling at me.

"So, you're here on contract, I presume, as you're not in the Paraguayan Air Force?"

"I am. A very long term and very lucrative one, I'm happy to say."

"So, who's flying the right seat? Did you bring someone down?"

He actually reddens, but then quickly offers, "No, no, I have a great co-pilot picked from their people."

That's getting me nowhere, so I press, "So, where were you from in the States?"

"I came down from the L.A. area. How about you?"

"Originally from Wyoming, lately from Las Vegas."

"I thought Paragon Avionics was based in Philadelphia."

Time to think fast again. "They are, but now with the internet and FedEx, hell, you can work almost anywhere."

Micha interrupts us. "I have a young pilot to check out this afternoon. If you want to see the Icon, we must hurry."

I rise and shake hands with Glascock. If he only knew I'd like to rip his arm off and beat him to death with it! But he doesn't. His time will come, particularly if he had anything to do with Bartlett being missing, and I'm sure he was in the middle of it.

As it's a quarter mile from the office to the Icon, G5, Citabria hangar, Micha jumps into a Toyota jeep and we screech out. He even drives like a hotshot pilot.

I study the hangar as much as I can as we approach. The guards are still in place, flanking the one hundred-forty-foot-wide hangar doors. There are video surveillance cameras on the front corners of the building, but I don't see any on the back. There's no obvious alarm system so I presume they depend on human guards.

After twenty minutes admiring the Icon, I head to the G5, but am called up short by Micha. "I have got to get back," he says.

"I've got to pee like a race horse," I say. "*Baños?*"

"*Pronto, por favor*," he says.

He points to a far corner of the hangar, luckily, I hope, a back corner, as far as it can be from the wide hangar doors, and I jog over. As I hoped, it has a window…and I promptly turn the latch, leaving it easily pushed open.

I wait a reasonable time, then exit and jog back, and we hurry out to the Toyota, and on the return I notice something I haven't before.

"Are those kennels over against that hangar?" I ask, hoping I'm wrong.

"Yes, we have a pair of guard dogs."

"But they seem to be locked up."

"Only used *en la noche*. At night, they roam free around the hangars," he says, and I have to sigh deeply.

Fuck, guard dogs. That makes things a little tougher.

The slight five hour change in time is catching up with me, or maybe it's the cognac, so when I'm let off at the steps of Hotel La Mision, I decide to head up and take a short nap before I call Carmen.

But it's not to be.

As I pass the desk, Sancho Alfonso, the hotel manager waves me over.

"Messages?" I ask.

"No, *Señor*. You asked me about a gentleman named Bartlett?"

"Yes, sir," I say, hopefully.

"I am sorry to inform you...." He hands me a photo copy of a newspaper article, and as I read, continues, "When you mentioned the name...well, it came to me after I returned home. I remembered because my grandfather was bitten by a banana spider when I was very young, and almost died."

I cannot get enough out of the article, written in Spanish, so I'm forced to ask him to read it to me.

"I will only read the high points, if you don't mind, as I'm very busy."

"Fine."

"Señor Tobias Bartlett, an American houseguest of Colonel Emilio Vargas, Paraguayan Air Force, was bitten by a banana spider, an *armadeiras* as we call them, in the night while in his bed at the Colonel's *estancia*...how do you say, farm or ranch?...and expired at the *Bautista*...Baptist Hospital. He was comatose when he arrived by ambulance and pronounced dead immediately. It's strange to note that Señor Bartlett was not in possession of a passport, and migra has no record of his entering the country...and although he was a guest of Colonel Vargas, no one knew of his next of kin. An investigation is underway and his demise will be reported to the American Embassy. This is an unusual death, as only fourteen deaths from *armadeiras* have been recorded."

"Mother fucker," I mumble.

"Pardon?" he replies.

"What's the date of the article?"

"Two weeks ago."

I call Carmen and ask her to either pick me up or I'll try and find Alex and send him to get her. She says she'll be at the hotel in forty-five minutes, but won't be driving, will cab it, so I call Alex to pick us both up in an hour.

While I'm waiting I put in another call to Pax. "Hey, buddy, I'm still not positive about the airplane and don't know if I'll be dead sure by in the morning."

"The boys are all scheduled to fly out tomorrow, per your instructions."

"Okay, okay, the airlines will fuck us to death if we try to change. Let 'em come. I'll do my best to see what's up with serial numbers...sometime tonight."

This is way too fishy for my taste, so I'm headed for the hospital to see who I can talk with. A spider, my ass.

Chapter Nineteen

Carmen merely shrugs her shoulders when I tell her about Bartlett's death, as if death is common enough in Paraguay, but she agrees to go with me to the hospital to talk to the doctors and whoever did an autopsy on him, if one was done.

We're not shown to the doctor who treated Bartlett or to the morgue and pathologist who did the autopsy. Instead, we're ushered into the hospital administrator's office. Señora Julieta Rejala is a short, buxom woman who charges around her large desk a little like a freight train. She shakes hands like a man, with both Carmen and me, then returns to her seat and leans forward on her forearms, all business.

First she turns to Carmen. "Have we not met before, Señorita?" she asks.

"Possibly. Although I've been in Estados Unidos for a few years."

"A fund raiser for the hospital, possibly?"

"Five or six years ago, if so. My father was here for an operation, and my uncle served on your board at one time."

"And he was?"

"Ricardo Juarez, brother of my father Alfonso and my other uncle, Manolo."

"Of course. Now," she turns her attention back to me, "what can I do for you?"

"You had a patient, Tobias Bartlett—"

"The victim of a spider bite, as I recall. We actually didn't have him in treatment as he was pronounced dead upon arrival."

"The newspaper—" I start to say.

"The newspaper is often wrong, and was wrong about that. He'd expired before the ambulance crew arrived at Colonel Vargas's home, and could not be revived."

"But was autopsied?" I ask.

"Of course. A physician was not in attendance at his death, and he was certainly not old enough to die of natural causes."

"May I have a copy of the autopsy?"

"And you're related to Señor Bartlett how?"

"No relation. I'm merely representing his wife."

"Aw, so he has relatives?"

"In California, a wife and two daughters. His wife, Penny, would like me to arrange to transport his body—"

"He was buried shortly after his death," she says, and looks a little too satisfied for my taste. Then she continues. "I'm sorry, but since you are not a relative, I am afraid I've already said too much."

"So, what do you need to give me all the pertinent reports and lab results?"

"A request from your embassy or a certified notarized letter from Mrs. Bartlett."

I'm not happy, but it's her rules, and I've got to play by them unless I can figure a way not to. As soon as we leave, we head for the embassy.

Theo Gann is in his office, and has us shown right in.

I introduce him to Carmen and he gives her a smile with lips tight as a gopher snake, and a caution, "I've read quite a bit about your fiancée, Mr. Reardon. Are you sure you know what you're getting yourself into?"

Carmen laughs. "Yes," and gives me an admiring glance. "He's an interesting fellow. A fellow who could use your help."

"Oh," Gann says. "He wasn't exactly cooperative when I called on him at the hotel."

I step into the conversation. "The hell you say, I bought your cup of tea."

"That you did," he says, and I get the snake lips. "So, what's up?"

"To be truthful, Carmen's family is only part of the reason I came to Paraguay. The other part was to help a friend locate her husband, and I'm afraid I did."

"This...husband...is an American citizen?"

"Was. I understand the embassy was informed of his death...Tobias Bartlett."

"I'd hear of the death of an American here in Paraguay and we have had no report of the death of any Tobias Bartlett."

I glance over at Carmen, then back to Gann. "Interesting. The newspaper and the hospital said the embassy had been informed."

"I guess there's a chance, and I'll check into it. If I learn anything, I'll give you a call. You still at La Mision?"

"Of course, if he was murdered, and the hospital, military, and maybe even the police were complicit, then you'd not be informed."

He laughs. "You sure you're not Clive Cussler or Agatha Christie or something? That's hardly likely unless you have proof of some kind?"

"No proof."

He's so smug I want to plaster his nose all over his face, as he snorts, "I didn't think so."

"I am still at La Mision, but there's more. I want a copy of his autopsy and his death certificate, and I'd like to interview the doctor who pronounced him."

"He has relatives in the states?"

"He does, a wife and children. I was on the phone with her yesterday."

"Have her contact State and have them request the info from me and give me permission to have you see it, and that can happen."

"Bullshit, Gann. That will take a month of Sundays."

"That's the way it works."

"So, I'm telling you that an American died in Paraguay, and, for sure, the embassy is supposed to be contacted—"

"We weren't."

"But you were supposed to be, and you were not, and of course you wouldn't be if there was some government involvement...so is that as far as it goes?"

"That's the way it works, Reardon." He climbs to his feet, walks to his door, and holds it for us. "Stay out of trouble," he says as I walk past.

Then I stop and turn. "He was a very nice young man, with a beautiful wife and children. She teaches school in California. Good family folks."

He shrugs, looking very bored.

So I continue, lowering my tone an octave. "And you're a total prick and I'd like to stomp your nuts into a grease spot right here on your chicken shit tile floor."

He steps back a couple of steps and holds his palms out. "We have security here, you know."

"Yeah, and being such a total dickhead, you probably need it a lot. And, sir, you are going to damn well need it if you don't pursue this."

He walks quickly back to his desk, and picks up the phone.

"I'm leaving, Gann," I say, "but I should shove that phone up your worthless ass."

Chapter Twenty

As we head to where Alex waits in the parking lot, Carmen earns her money. "My Uncle Ricardo knows everyone in that hospital, where he was once a board member, and he hates corruption and hates incompetence even more. I've heard him speak badly of Señora Rejala. May I ask him to help?"

"May you? Damn right you may."

"Then I will. Are we dining tonight? Another trip to Bolsi?"

"I'd love to but I have an errand I have to run."

"Without your interpreter?" she asks, playfully.

"Yes, ma'am. I've got to go his one alone."

"You're not...how do I ask this politely...you're not taking advantage of our dark side are you, my fiancée," she says, then giggles.

"I haven't visited a whorehouse, if that's what you're asking, since I was sixteen."

"Good. Then I will sleep peacefully."

We drop her at a shopping center, at her direction, and then I'm alone with Alex, and ask, "You want to pick up a half million of those guarani of yours?"

"Of course, Señor. Who do you want to disappear into the swamp?" he asks, but laughs, and it's all I can do not to give him Theo Gann's name. Instead, I say, "I need come black clothes, some *soldado* outfits. You know, night gear. Like the guards at the airport wear. Then I need you to drive me tonight, and wait, and ask no questions."

"That is much to ask. Will this get me to the *jusgados*...how do you say, jail?"

"It could, if you think I'm the kind of man who'll get caught. But this kind of work is my job, has long been my job, and I don't plan to get caught, or get you caught, as I plan for it to be my job for a long, long time to come. And, *mi amigo*, all you have to do is wait."

He's silent for a moment, then glances back over his shoulder. "Then a million guarani wouldn't be out of the question?"

"You're a hard man, Alex. How about seven hundred thou?"

"How about a million, Señor. I have a wife and children who will starve if papa is in the *jusgado*...and half in advance, of course."

"Of course," I say and laugh—realizing a million guarani, at forty-five hundred to the dollar, is just a little over two hundred twenty bucks—as he heads for a store that looks to be sporting goods.

I brought a pair of hiking boots so it was nothing but pants and shirt needed. Even my jungle camo has some light spots, and for this job, it's night fighter gear. I pick out a few other select items and we take our leave.

Happy that I'm able to fill my little shopping list, I return to the car and I instruct Alex to find a pharmacy. He does and I'm able to cross off another item on my list.

When I pass the desk, carrying my shopping bag full of clothes, Señor Alfonso again waves me over. "Señor, the gentleman, Señor Glascock, our former guest, stopped by to see you. He's waiting on the patio having a cocktail...his fourth. Would you like me to bring you one and join him?"

"Yeah, tall vodka tonic, squeeze of lime, please." I need to be on my best later tonight, so I'm taking it real easy. I'm a little taken aback, as the last person I thought would give me a social call was good old Charlie Glascock, but I'm more than eager to have a chat with him. I'd prefer the chat was somewhere in a dark alley, but I'll get around to that.

"Hey, Reardon," he says with a friendly smile as I approach. He pulls a chair out next to him, both of us shaded by a wide green umbrella in the center of the glass table.

I sit, and ask, "Hey, I thought you weren't interested in any avionics?"

"Just a social call. Not too many gringos around to chat with."

"Oh, I get the impression that Colonel Vargas talks a lot more gringo than he lets on."

"You think so?" he says, then laughs. "He's a cagey son-of-a-bitch, and does understand damn near everything that goes on around him, so you're probably right."

Alfonso arrives with my drink, and Glascock leans over and pulls my shopping bag open. "Black? Hell man, you're in the tropics."

I give him a smile that I hope is not as phony-looking as it feels. "Yeah, but sometimes you got to go formal, and I've been invited to dinner at a beautiful *estancia*. Got to look sharp." I move the sack to my other side so he doesn't look any deeper.

I sip my drink, then ask, "So, where's the hot club action around town?"

"Hell, I don't need it. The colonel has provided me with a place overlooking the river and a couple of girls who tend to all my needs...and I mean all." He guffaws.

"Hell? Sounds like heaven to me."

I guess he thinks he's bullshitted me enough, and his smile disappears. "So, Reardon, why are you really in Asuncion? You CIA or some cockamamie horseshit like that? You look ex-military to me."

"Marine, years ago. Civilian for a long time...nothing to do with Uncle Sam." Time to lie again. "I was crew chief on some jump jets...where I got some of my avionics training."

"I don't think so." He's eying me through furrowed brows.

"Hey, I'm just settling into this job. If I'd been at things as long as an old fart like you, I'd probably be better at it."

He's not amused. He shoots the rest of his drink, then rises. "Well, I thought I might drop by and say howdy...so, howdy. I've got to go see what my two housekeepers are up to."

"I feel real sorry for you," I say with a laugh, and rise and stick my hand out. He shakes with a limp-dick handshake, then heads for the lobby and out the front door.

As I flop down on my bed to take a rest, I'm wondering just what brought Glascock to my door. I hope he has no idea I'm working for Wedgeworth. If he has any inkling there'll be a welcoming party at the airport. I'm wondering if I should wait until the boys arrive and I have lots of firepower, since they're coming anyway. I decide, to hell with it, maybe they'll get in just in time to spring me out of the *jusgados* rather than help me recover the plane.

I'm going tonight.

I check my phone before I close my eyes and see I have a text from Pax with the arrival time of Skip Allen, Hank Hausman, Everete 'Wetback' Alvarez and Chad 'Madman' Madsen, and see it's not until eleven thirty PM, same flight as I came in on. There's also a call from the beautiful Tatya Bolinsky, Wedgeworth's secretary, with a two word message "Miss you"; and one from Tenee Wedgeworth, his daughter, and it's a little disturbing. She says, "I told you I need to get out of here and if you were the tough guy you look like, you'd help us. I think you're an asshole, just like my old man."

She said "us" like she meant both her and her little sister. Something's weird about that family, and I'm beginning to wonder if it's not more than just mama's boozing it up.

When I've got my recovery fee, and gee whiz Wedgeworth has no more hammer over my head, I'll dig deeper into that aspect of my new friendship with the Wedgeworths.

I set the alarm on my iPhone for nine fifteen and decide to get some shuteye, just as my phone goes off with an unknown caller.

It's Carmen. "Hey, I got your autopsy report in hand, and even some pictures of poor Mr. Bartlett. And it seems he did die of a spider bite."

"How about brunch in the morning? Here at the hotel? I can send a cab for you."

"Cabs are nothing, here. What time?"

"Ten AM, I know you like to sleep in. And bring the report."

"Okay, big boy, but no hanky-panky. I'm saving it for the wedding night." She laughs healthily, then says "*mañana*" and hangs up.

I'm too wound up to sleep, so I gather my gear and call down to room service. "Two pounds of raw steak, please."

"Pardon?"

"Yes, two pounds of raw steak. To the room, please."

Chapter Twenty One

I take the stairs down from my third floor room and exit via a back way, then work my way around to the front.

While I'm waiting for Alex to arrive—standing outside the hotel where I've slunk back into the tall shrubbery to be inconspicuous, dressed in black from head to toe, with a small bug-out bag in hand, sipping a cup of coffee—I decide to text both Tatya and Tenee. Tatya gets a "Working hard, getting Prather K's ride back. See you soon." And then to Tenee, "Sorry I'm not there. Out of the country. We'll talk soon."

Alex is right on time and seems a little nervous as he roars away from the curb. And even more nervous when I tell him to head for the airport.

"Slow down, Alex," I command. "Don't break any traffic laws."

"What you got in the bag?" He asks.

"Tools of my trade."

"Señor, you are not a terrorist are you?"

I laugh, hoping to relax him a little. "No, Alex. I'm merely doing a little company spying. My company is interested in some new products manufactured by another company, and your airport is way ahead of other places and has some installed. I'm just taking some pictures, but can't be seen doing it."

"Oh, company espionage, I have heard of that."

"That's it." He seems to relax, and slows a little.

Then he glances back over his shoulder, again worriedly. "Why you did not do this in the States?"

"Well, it's a crime in the United States for one company to spy on another company. I had to go outside of the U.S. to do so. Paraguay doesn't give a damn about one American company spying on another."

"Ahh, that makes very much sense."

I have no idea if it's true or makes any sense at all, but it sounds good, and he relaxes even more. I have him drop me off a half-mile beyond the Air Force buildings, but still inside the separately fenced Air Force complex, where the fence is lined with brush between fence and road, and wave at him as he drives away with instructions to return in two hours. The fence is eight feet high with three strands of barb wire topping it, but I see no reason to climb. I work my way into the brush, dig out my cutters, and begin working my wire clippers, opening a five-foot gash in the cyclone wire. I slip inside, dig a two foot long strip of white cloth out of my bug-out bag, and tie it two feet off the ground so I can find the damn thing, even at a dead run.

I've picked this spot because there's a thirty-foot tower between it and the hangars, with some type of avionics equipment mounted on its top. I hustle to it, dig another tool out of the bag, and climb about ten feet up its ladder. Then I put my little implement to work. It's a simple tool—a whistle, with a tone above what a human can hear. I'm wondering if it's working, then am sure it is, as I hear violent barking. I'm rewarded with two very large German Shepherds, kicking dirt out behind, coming my way like I'm a t-bone steak...which I'm not, but I do have two nice chunks of sirloin in my bag and dig them out. They are each laced with four nice sleeping pills, and as soon as the dogs quit jumping as high as they can, trying to get a bite out of any part of me, they settle to a low growl, each looking up at me as if I'm the interloper I am. I throw one chunk to the left and one to the right.

Oops! Both of them inspect the steaks, but don't attack them as I anticipated they would. Instead, they return to below my perch and continue the low growl.

The best laid plans of mice and stupid men. What now?

I decide to convince them of my innocence and helplessness, and begin to sing a couple of low Irish lullabies my sainted mama taught me. If that doesn't piss them off, I don't know what will, and if anyone's heard my singing, they'd understand, but strangely enough, after five or six nice slow versions, on the third repeat they stop growling and one of them actually sinks to his belly. He keeps glancing up at me, but at least he's relaxed. My singing would bore anything, including a slathering beast.

It's at least a half hour, and my voice is beginning to go with the tenth repeat, when the mutt still standing walks over and settles to his belly in front of the steak, plops one paw on it, and begins gnawing. Thankfully, it's more than the other mutt can stand and he attacks the other chunk.

It's another twenty minutes before both are snoring like a pair of lumberjacks and I'm able to dismount the tower. I like dogs, and hope I haven't overdosed them. I have no idea how long they'll be out, and I damn sure want to be long gone when they come to. They looked mean as hell, and I imagine they'll be even meaner with a sleeping pill hangover.

I have to quarter around to approach the G5 hangar from the rear, where I believe there are no surveillance cameras and I'm out of sight of the guards stationed at the huge sliding doors. Search as I may, I see no cameras, and quickly find the *baños* window I've unlatched. I'm inside in a heartbeat and crack the door just enough to peer in, see no one, crack it more, and stick my head in enough to really survey the big space.

I pause long enough to screw a suppressor on the Glock, just in case.

The two smaller planes are between me and the G5, and I weave through them until I'm beside the beautiful aircraft. Even in the semi-darkness, it's obvious why someone would want to own, even steal, such an incredible piece of equipment. My manual says there's a serial number located on the landing gear, which, of course, is down, and I have my head up in the wheel well when I hear a door open.

I bang my head trying to extricate myself, and it rings across the room like someone has struck a base drum. I plaster myself up against the side of a tire and hold my breath.

How can I not be fucked, fried, and fricasseed?

Chapter Twenty Two

It's both guards, carrying Hechler and Koch's HK416 fully automatics, and me with my lousy Glock. But they're not panning a light, or their muzzles, around the room, or turning on the main overhead lamps. They stand just inside the door and one produces a bottle that's been hidden in a trash can, and they take turns taking deep draws from it.

I guess what sounded like a car wreck to me was not quite so loud to two drunks. Maybe they're used to the metal hangar popping and cracking with the change in temperature. They laugh, exchanging some lurid tale, then pass the bottle again, killing it, and drop it into the trash—this time, I presume it's final resting place. And then they're gone.

Finally, I can breathe. I did not find the serial number I was looking for, so I switch on my pen light again and start back into the wheel well. Then I realize there is something I hadn't noticed. The new blue paint job only wraps partially up into the wheel well and the original white paint extends well beyond. A sloppy job these South Americans did. It makes me smile.

I can't find the damn serial number. It's get inside the engine cowlings, or inside the plane, if I'm to find other serial numbers on my list. I have a Leatherman tool, but have no idea if it'll work in whatever fasteners they use on the engine cowlings, or even if I can lift the damn things alone, but I decide to give it a look.

The G5 enjoys twin engines mounted aft either side of the fuselage, just ahead of the tail and high off the ground, so I'll need a ladder. It's seconds before I find a rolling twelve-foot ladder stowed up against the hangar wall, and only a minute or so before I have it plane-side and am mounting it, when the roar of electric motors stops me cold and I see the huge hangar doors beginning to part. There's no time to move the ladder—just time to haul ass and I hit the ground in a jump and take four strides. Light floods the place, and I've no place to hide.

I'm beside the Citabria. I pop the door and cram myself low enough that I can't be seen unless someone peers in.

I hear footfalls and pray they're not coming for a little joy ride in the stunt plane; then I hear a voice raised in anger. It's my old buddy Charlie Glascock.

"Goddamit, Marcos, I asked you to check things out before you left. You dumb fuck, you didn't notice a fucking ladder in front of the stabilizer?"

"It was not there when I left, Señor Glascock."

"Right, you dumb fuck. Get the tractor and get her out. We've got to taxi over to the fucking office as the General is too lazy to drive over here. Let's go, let's go."

"It is Rio, Señor?"

"Yes. We're just dropping his party off, then we return as the colonel has a flight this weekend. We're headed to Lima for a week."

"*Si.*"

That is bad news. I have no interest in hanging around Paraguay for a couple of weeks waiting for a shot at the G5. I've got to step it up.

It probably takes twenty minutes before I hear the doors roll shut again and the lights dim. I got a frigging cramp, all balled up in the little Citabria, curled around the stick, and I have to walk around the two smaller planes twice to shake it off.

Now, if only the frigging killer dogs haven't come to. I glance at my watch and realize it's been just over two hours since I watched Alex drive away.

I hope the dogs are still out, and I hope Alex has some leeway in his fat black heart.

I get far enough out of the lights illuminating the tarmac around the hangar taxiways and then begin a dead run for the fence, passing the sleeping dogs. As the saying goes, I let them lie. They don't twitch as I pound by. I hope I haven't killed them.

As I'd hoped, the white cloth I tied on the fence is blowing in the wind and I find it easily. I'm out of the Air Force compound. So far, so good.

But, as I worried, there is no cab parked nearby.

I wait ten minutes, then decide I can walk the two or three miles to the airport terminal and catch a cab there. But finally I see lights approaching. I step back into the brush, as it's coming fast; then it slows to a crawl and almost idles along, and I realize it has Taxi Benitez painted on the driver's door. I jump out of the brush and he slams on his brakes.

In seconds, we're rolling toward the hotel.

"You're a rich man, Alex," I say.

"I have lost ten pounds worrying," he says, and I can hear the stress in his voice.

"You can spare it."

"When do I get the rest of my money?"

"When you deposit me back at the hotel, unless you want dollars."

"*Bueno. Bueno. Bueno.* Guarani, *por favor.* I want nothing more to do with *Norte Americanos.* No offense, Señor. "

"None taken, Alex. You did a good job. I'm going to throw in a little more, as you waited for me and I was late."

"Bueno. Bueno. Bueno."

I'm feeling pretty damn good. Even though I didn't get a serial number, I did determine that the plane was formerly white.

I'm feeling pretty damn good, that is, until I walk to the desk to change my dollars for guarani and the manager, Señor Angelo, looks up, sees me, and gets very wide eyed. "Señor, the *policia*, the worst of them, former Pyragüés, were here, and tore your room...our room...to pieces. You owe us several hundred dollars for damages. And I must call them and inform them you've returned."

"What the hell did they want?"

"You, Señor. They wanted you."

"Well, Señor Angelo, if you want your several hundred dollars, you'll not call them until I've checked the room, packed what's there, and left. Understand?"

"I must call."

"Fine," I wave a handful of bills at him. "No time, *no dinero, amigo.*"

"Go and pack. I will not call until you return."

"You'll go with me. I'll pack. I'll pay you. I'll leave. Then you can call. Tell them I came in a rear door, unseen. "

He nods, exits the desk, and follows me to the elevator.

As we're waiting, I ask, "What's this Pyragüés?"

"Secret police. They no longer call themselves that, but that's who they are. Murderers, thieves, rapers of women and children. The worst of Paraguay from the time of Stroessner. It literally means hairy footed in Guaraní. Why they are called that I have no idea...but I don't want their hairy foot on my neck."

The room has been turned upside down, but nothing is gone. I quickly pack my bag, and we're out of there. I settle with him for the room charges, plus five hun for the damages, change a grand in dollars for Paraguayan currency, and am happy that Alex is waiting patiently for his money.

I climb in and pay him what he's owed, plus another hundred and twenty thousand, then ask: "Okay, you sure you don't want more of *Norte Americanos*? Another million more, to be exact?"

Chapter Twenty Three

I give Alex my best all American boy smile. "Hey, *amigo*, all you got to do is drive me and keep the *policia* from chucking me in some deep hole. Hell, if they catch us, I'll tell them you're just another *gordo* cab driver. *Capisce*?"

"What is this, *capisce*?"

"Sorry, Alex, wrong language. *Comprendo*?"

"*Si*, I understand. Another million is not enough if the *policia* are after you."

"Okay, okay, how about a million and a quarter?"

"Two million, señor, half in advance, *porfavor*?"

"You're killing me here, *amigo*. How about a million and a half. We gotta get out of here."

"Okay, as soon as I get my million advance."

"Go, go, I'll count it out. You gotta take dollars."

He starts away, but not in a hurry, turns a corner, then pulls up. "How do I know it is the right amount?"

"Alex, it's two hundred twenty five bucks, okay?"

"What is this 'bucks?"

"A nickname for an American dollar."

"What is 'nickname?"

"Another name for something."

"So, a bucks is a dollar and a dollar is how many guarani?"

"Four thousand five hundred. Two hundred and twenty five dollars is a little more than a million guarani. Can we go now?"

"Okay, but do not call me fat...*gordo*." He begins to idle away. We only go another block before a red light flashing, siren screaming police car roars by, followed closely by two more plain black Mercedes four door late models. It seems the Pyragües, the hairy footed boys, travel in style.

"Is that for you?" he asks.

"No, no, probably some bank robber. Head out north of town."

"*Si, señor*. My dollars please."

I hand them over the seat and he stuffs them in a pocket.

As he winds his way through town, I grab my cell and call Carmen.

"Oh, hello Angelina," she answers, speaking English. "Sorry, I can't talk now, some gentlemen from the government are here. Can you call back in a half hour?" She's quiet for a moment, even though I say nothing, then adds, "Okay, a half hour." And hangs up. It seems the Pyragües are very busy boys. More importantly, it seems Carmen is still on my team. I'm wondering if they're thinking it's suspicious she's speaking in English, and it seems they are, as my phone buzzes before I can get it back in my pocket, and I see it's Carmen calling—most likely some prick who's grabbed her phone. I turn it off. Thank God I don't have a personal answering message. I'd like to chuck it out the window, but it's my lifeline, other than email, to Pax and the boys on their way down.

So I give Alex new instructions. "Stop anywhere I can buy a cell phone."

"*Si, Señor*. It is late, but I know a place."

Still, I have to worry about the Pyragüés being able to track my iPhone so I wait until he stops and go into settings and turn off everything but the vibrate. Hopefully, that will stall them, no matter how tech savvy they might be.

After buying a throwaway phone, and as we near the Juarez estancia, I ask Alex to pull off the road and park. It's just about forty-five minutes since I last called Carmen, but I want to wait a full hour just to be safe. We sit, and Alex nervously smokes a cigarette.

She doesn't bother with hello. "We can talk, they are gone."

"Obviously I'm in a little trouble," I say.

"When you are being searched for by the Special Police, formerly known as the Pyragüés, you are in more than a little trouble. They are much like your SWAT teams...but without morals or oversight."

"Can you meet me somewhere?"

"And where are you now?"

I have no idea how much I can trust her, so I lie. "I'm downtown. Where can we meet?"

"There's a park about halfway out of town coming to my uncle's. Revolución, it's called. It's nicely lighted, even this late. There's a statute of soldiers in the middle. I'll meet you there in...can you get there in twenty minutes?"

"Sure," I say, knowing it's only a mile back from where we're parked.

"Mike...what did you do?"

"Trespass, is all. I didn't steal anything,"—*yet, I think, but don't say*—"or kill anyone, or rob a bank."

"Twenty minutes."

I stay a quarter mile away, watching her approach in the same car her uncle picked us up from the airport, studying the whole area with my binoculars. The park is well lit, with mercury vapor lights surrounding the entire square block and spotlights on the statue in the center. If she's being followed, they are very, very good, as I can spot no tail. If someone is hiding in the car, she's parked over a hundred yards from the statue, so they'll have to move very fast to get close to me.

I have Alex drive me to the far side of the park, away from the main highway, and let me out. I give him instructions to wait out of easy sight but never to take his eyes off me. If he sees me break into a run toward the street, he's to pick me up and be ready to earn his million by getting away quickly.

He agrees, but looks like he's eaten something rotten and it's about to come back up.

She's already seated when I sidle up next to her and flop down on the wooden bench near the statues.

To my surprise and pleasure, she throws her arms around me, settles her face into the side of my neck, and whispers, "I was so very worried about you. You won't be so handsome if the Pyragüés catch up with you."

I shrug.

"Please, please," she pleads, "don't take them lightly. Now, what have you done to get half the country looking for you?"

Again, I shrug. "I trespassed on the airport property."

"They have video of you...or they think it's you...breaking into an Air Force hangar. They found their guard dogs unconscious—"

"They're okay, I hope?"

"They woke up a few hours after they were discovered and are fine."

"Good. So they are not positive it was me?"

"Not absolutely. But the American pilot...Señor Glascock they said...he said he was sure it was you. Mike, you don't want the Pyragüés questioning you. Men have been driven mad when in their custody for a few days."

"I get it."

"I can help you get out of the country."

"Did you bring the reports from the hospital?"

"And pictures...when can you leave for the border?" She hands me a letter size yellow envelope as we talk.

I smile. "My work's not done here. And I'll find my own way out of the country. I don't want you involved any more than you already are. I can't believe it's not you in the hands of the Pyragüés."

"My family is fairly well known, and fairly powerful, so it would have to be very, very, very serious for them to arrest me. I've never mentioned it to you, but my former husband is a senator."

"Aww, so he still protects you?"

This time it's her turn to smile. "I know where all the Diaz bodies are buried...and that's not a metaphor, it's a fact. And he knows I'm not stupid enough to keep that knowledge to myself. It's in the hands of others in my family. If something happens to me, his past will be in every paper in the country, and proof of his misdeeds on the desk of every policeman."

"So he's afraid not to protect you. Remind me to give my buddy Pax a pat on his ugly head for finding you."

"I will, and who would ever guess that we'd end up engaged." She laughs.

"It's been my pleasure." This time I take her cheeks between my hands and plant a big wet one right on her beautiful lips. It's all I can do not to try for a little tongue, but that might be pushing it, as I never know just how much she might be kidding, she kisses me back, then gives me that healthy laugh of hers. She's on her feet, waving over her shoulders as she heads back to uncle's car.

"You're still on the payroll," I yell after her.

She shouts over her shoulder, "Damn right I am. Call me if you need anything." And she's gone. I meander back to the side of the park where Alex is parked a hundred yards up a side road. He sees me coming, fires up the cab, and by the time I reach the roadside so does he.

"*Donde, Señor*? Where?"

"Let's head out of town, away from all these nasty police, and find a place where we can have a *cervesa* and something to eat to kill some time until we have to be back at the airport."

"You are leaving?"

"No, we're picking someone up."

"There are many police at the airport."

"Good, then you'll drive better."

"I drive perfect."

"Then drive me to somewhere we can watch the stars and get a beer."

"Then the airport?"

"Then the airport. Then we're going to Ciudad del Este."

That one drops his chin to his chest, then he recovers and stammers, "Ciudad del Este is five hours, five hours…if the roads are good."

"You are going to be a very rich man by the time my work is finished."

"Or a dead man."

"Not on my watch, *Señor*, not on my watch. It's another million for tomorrow."

"Plus petrol?" he asks.

Chapter Twenty Four

Alex, needless to say, is a little taken aback when four big guys walk out of the terminal, each with a duffle bag half their size.

He glares at me under chubby brows. "This is not someone, Señor, this is many someones."

"Probably too many for one vehicle. Do you know another cabby...one we can trust?"

"Of course, my cousin, Alfredo."

"Alex and Alfredo, sounds like a vaudeville or SNL team."

"Vaudeville?" he asks.

"Call your cousin."

I only have two weapons—not that I want to involve the pilot and co-pilot in any gunfight, but still, they have a right to defend themselves if things get rough.

It's after midnight by the time Alfredo arrives, and I send Wetback, Madman, and Hank Hausman with him to the Crowne Plaza in central Asuncion with instructions to lay low, stay out of trouble, and under no circumstance to call attention to themselves. I know they'll be tired from traveling and tonight won't be a problem. Tomorrow is another question as it'll take Skip and me at least until tomorrow night to get to Ciudad del Este, make contact with the guys Pax has located, get some weapons so we have a fighting chance if we come up against someone determined to take us down, and get back.

They all yawn and assure me that trouble is not on their menu, and we part company.

Alex, Skip and I start out to cross the country to the tri-border region, where Paraguay, Argentina, and Brazil meet. It's an interesting place, at least if all I've read is true. Over twenty thousand middle eastern immigrants reside there, most from Syria and Lebanon. It's reputed to be a major fundraising area for Hizbollah, Hamas and al Qaeda with arms for drugs, and drugs for arms with the Muslims trading with secular Latin American terrorist groups like the Revolutionary Armed Forces of Columbia, *Sendero Luninosos*—Shining Path of Peru—and others. The CIA believes over ten billion bucks a year funnel through the area.

Just the kind of place a couple of Iraq vets should be very, very unwelcome.

As we exit the Asuncion metropolitan area, Alex whines. "I cannot drive all night, Señor."

"You won't have to. Skip and I will take over when you get tired. But drive a while, as I have some reading to do."

For the first time, I open the envelope Carmen has provided, with photos and reports, only some of which I understand. The bite was to the back of his neck, and the inflammation, based on what I can see in the pictures, is nothing less than horrible. As terrible as it is, I find a section that makes me laugh, and Skip, beside me in the back seat, looks over.

"What the hell is funny about an autopsy report?" he asks.

"Did you know that the bite of the banana spider, a phoneutria or some bullshit scientific name, gives you a constant hard-on, to the point of it being painful?"

"No," he says, "that's a bit of trivia I did not know. So, did he die from erectus gigantias?"

"No, he died of a spider bite, or so this report says…but I'm sure that's total bullshit. Either that, or he was held down while someone pushed a spider down on his neck until Mr. Spider took umbrage and bit the shit out of him."

"I wonder if they have to bury you in a closed coffin if you have a giant hard-on?"

"Now it's you being funny."

"Keep reading, I'm gonna nap."

"Good." And I do. I study the pictures, including one of the actual fang marks, taken with a centimeter ruler in the shot. I'm a little surprised to see fang marks that are over a centimeter apart. This must have been a very, very large spider.

I tire of trying to decipher the reports, and of looking at the pics of a guy who, from all I can discover, was a very nice young man with a very nice family.

Now that dipshit Glascock has ratted me out, I have one more reason to do the son-of-a-bitch. The more I look at the pics of Toby Bartlett, who obviously died a horrible painful death, the less I give a rat's ass about who gets in the way of my stealing the airplane. I really don't want to have to shoot down a bunch of Air Force guards who are merely doing their job, and will try my very best to avoid such, but I am going to take the G5 out of Paraguay…hell or high water.

As we begin to see more and more lights, I pull off and wake Alex, not trusting my own driving on tight crowded streets.

It's well after midnight when we crawl into Ciudad del Este, a city of over three hundred thousand—the second largest in Paraguay—to the west of the Brazilian and Paraguayan border, which is the Parayan River. Even now the traffic is near a standstill. I've read that the dope smugglers rule the night and the river is not patrolled, as it would be too dangerous.

Adjacent on the Brazilian side of the river is the city of Foz do Iguacu, equally large. Like most South American cities, it is a contrast of modern buildings and slums. My reading has illustrated that it's a city of crime, with Chinese, Russians, Syrians, Lebanese, Koreans, and of course Brazilians, Argentinians and Paraguayans. There are far more casinos and whorehouses than churches, although in the few blocks we've travelled it's the prevalence of Sunnis and Shiites is obvious which is to be expected with over twenty thousand Muslims in the triple border region. There's even the occasional pagoda.

A good portion of Paraguay's economy stems from the sale of power from the Itapiu Dam, located just north adjoining the city, which backs up a huge body of water, Republic Lake. The river below is at least a half-mile wide.

Ciudad del Este appears to be the underbelly of three countries, and the belly hair is infested with sand fleas from the Near East.

The names I've been given by Pax are both Middle Eastern—Abad Itanid and Hasaan Al-Farashi, both well-known arms dealers. I'm told I can find Al-Farashi at or near the Mosque of the Prophet Muhammad, where a spice shop fronts for his dope and arms smuggling operation. Itanid is located across the river, a farmer, whose coffee plantation is small but obviously profitable, or at least it would seem so as his *estancia* is two storey with a large indoor pool. The real operation, however, is deep in the jungle, accessible only by foot, and coffee is not the crop. Coca is the primary crop, for the production of cocaine, and cannabis the secondary. It's again amazing to me what Pax can dig out of the web.

Too bad he couldn't dig up a nice ex-patriot American arms dealer whose first inclination would not be tacking my hide to his trophy wall.

Chapter Twenty Five

Alex works his way to the mosque, seemingly a new building. We find a parking spot across the street in front of a coffee house and café, The Alhambra, and decide to sleep the night away, of which there's very little left.

It's not an easy place to sleep—cramped in a car, lots of traffic noise, a populace who would slit your throat upon learning you'd fought in Iraq. It's particularly uncomfortable for Skip, who's six-feet-five and over two hundred and fifty pounds. No matter how cramped, he sleeps.

Dawn finds the coffee shop still closed, but the traffic is even thicker—bumper to bumper—and most of them obviously think the horn will clear the way. Even with the noise, Alex and Skip manage to sleep on, but I decide to walk. Before I circle the first block, I come upon Abad's Spices, if my Spanish is any good...*Especia* Abad. I pass a dozen street vendors stocking their stalls with Armani and Gucci purses, the latest movies on CD, and electronics with Apple and Sony labels...the rip off of all the great names. Where else can you get a Gucci handbag for twenty bucks?

The spice shop has yet to open, but I suspect it will soon as the lights are on in what appears to be a home-over-business.

By the time I circle three more blocks and return to the car, both Skip and Alex are standing outside watching the traffic go by while Alex begs a cancer with a morning smoke and Skip playfully negotiates with a five foot tall, five-foot-round street vendor, made taller by the red fez with black tassel he wears, for a faux Rolex.

"Coffee?" I ask.

"Coffee, hell," Skip replies. "A few hotcakes, some pork chops and scrambled eggs."

I have to laugh at that one. "You damn sure won't get any pork chops in this neighborhood."

"Yeah, I forgot. Okay, yogurt and some good *pan dulce*."

I wave for them to follow and we're in the café in ten steps.

Over coffee, bread hot from the oven, goat cheese and fresh fruit, I ask Alex, "Okay, what time will the spice shop open? Especia Abad is only a half block around the corner, and it's the only spice shop for four blocks around, if my walk told me anything."

"Maybe eight, maybe nine…or maybe ten. *Quien sabe*."

"Who knows," I reply. He's a wealth of information.

After we finish eating and head that way, I turn to Skip. "Hey, I want you to stay out of sight. We may need some element of surprise with this bunch. No reason to lay all our cards on the table."

"I'll hang back," he says and stops to window-shop a couple of doors from the spice shop.

"I stay with Señor Skip?" Alex asks.

"No, you stay with me. You translate."

"Okay, maybe more bucks?"

"Maybe a kick in the ass."

That quiets him. The shop is open and a tall man in a striped disdasha is behind the counter sorting small bags of some yellow substance.

"Abad?" I ask, and he looks me up and down carefully before answering.

"No, Señor Itanid is the owner and only here occasionally," Alex translates.

"Where may I find him?" I ask.

"He works at his warehouse and does not like to be bothered."

"I need to speak with him."

"About?"

"About buying some items from him."

"What items?"

"Personal, but it involves a great deal of money."

"Your name?" he asks.

"Strong. Richard Strong," I lie.

He nods, and walks to the back of the shop, out of earshot, and dials on his cell phone. In moments, he walks back and hands me the phone, which I pass to Alex.

"Señor Itanid wishes to know exactly what it is you wish to purchase."

I hesitate a moment, wondering how to phrase it, then offer "War surplus."

And it seems Alex is getting directions.

As we drive south along the wide river, I'm amazed at how many well-armed police and soldiers I see along the roadways. Almost every corner as we drive out of town has at least one policeman or soldier with both an automatic slung beneath an arm and a sidearm. And I see many in street clothes carrying what appear to be full automatics. This place is definitely the wildwest.

After twenty minutes of winding our way through town, the crowded city spreads a little, and becomes more industrial.

When we're a block from the high fence surrounding a yard and the Itanid warehouse, we drop Skip off with instructions to stay out of sight but stand by in case we get in trouble.

We slow and turn into a fenced yard with a gate just inside, with a guard. Alex speaks to him. I note the sidearm he wears under an un-tucked t-shirt, and he walks over and swings the gate aside. I'd think it a scrap yard, but in fact the vehicles are all of military origin, most old and beat to hell, but a couple of fairly new halftracks. None of them have weapons mounted where they once might have been.

The structure in the distance must cover most of an acre, maybe a hundred feet wide by four hundred long. It appears to be adobe, or maybe plaster over concrete blocks. A guard is seated outside a pass-through alongside sliding doors large enough to accommodate any vehicle in the yard.

He rises from a ladder-back chair and keeps a hand on a weapon on his belt. We exit, Alex speaks to him, and he waves us through.

My eyes immediately settle on a round table near the door to an inside office, where four bearded men sit, some smoking, some drinking tea or coffee, all with either sidearms or an AK47 leaning close at hand. They are fat and skinny, one is bald and one has hair and beard black and curly as a steel wool; another has hair and beard ruler straight.

The warehouse smells of spices, but some of the cases I see stacked in the distance, all painted black which I imagine is to occlude any markings. Their appearance whiffs of crated weapons and a few look to be the exact size to house an RPG—rocket propelled grenade—case.

One of the bearded men rises and waves us toward the interior office door. The inside is divided into two offices, the outer one with a young male with a Hollywood five-day beard behind a desk, the floors covered with what appear to be Persian carpets, the walls with pictures of Mecca and mosques. There's not a Playboy pinup to be seen.

The young man circles the desk and indicates to me to hold my arms out, then frisks me and relieves me of my Ruger from its holster in the small of my back. I allow it. He frisks Alex as well, who looks as if he's swallowed a frog and sounds so as he croaks "*Pardon, por favor*," and turns and heads back out the door. The young man stops him and points to a chair against the wall, and Alex sits as carefully as if he was about to hatch eggs. As soon as he's seated, the young man instructs him—presume to stay seated—then returns to me and holds the inner office door open.

A portly gentleman, bald except for a thick beard, is behind a metal desk shuffling papers. A smoking gold colored hookah, a water pipe with a long tube, rests on the edge of his desk but the smoke smells like tobacco, not cannabis. The room is barren except for two wooden chairs and a hat rack. The fat man looks up, and rolls of suet stick out on the back of his skull and neck. He doesn't rise, then asks as he continues shuffling papers, "Señor Strong? I speak English."

"Yes, sir."

"You are an American?"

"I am."

"Why does an American come to Paraguay to buy war surplus?"

"This American cannot buy war surplus...weapons ...in America, and cannot fly with them to South America...or anywhere else. And I have business in Brazil that requires weapons."

"And who says I have weapons to sell?"

"I have my sources."

He eyes me carefully, like a mongoose eyeing a cobra, then says, slowly and carefully, "If your sources are American spies, you will find yourself in our incinerator and your mother will begin to wonder why you have not called home."

I laugh, even though I don't find him particularly humorous. "If I knew American spies they would be after me, even more than you."

"So, you are a mercenary?"

"Let's leave it at the fact that I have a need for arms and I'm willing to pay good money for them."

"And what would you think an AK47 worth?"

"How about five hundred dollars...U.S.?"

"You only need a single weapon, it would be a thousand U.S., but I will throw in five hundred rounds of ammunition."

"I need five, so five hundred is a good price. And I want one of those RPG's you have in crates painted black."

He smiles tightly. "An RPG would be against the law of every country in South America and your part of the Americas as well, I would imagine."

"True," I say, and smile. "So, are the ones you have 18's or the reloadable 16's?"

"16's."

"So, how much?"

"Three thousand five hundred."

"I'll give you six thousand for the lot. Five AK47's with five hundred rounds each, two thirty shot clips with each, no tracers, one RPG with five reloads."

"I would consider eight thousand, no less."

"Make it an even seven thousand and you have a deal."

"I am not a rug merchant, Señor Strong. But I will consider seven thousand five hundred."

"Fine," I reach across the desk to shake hands.

He smiles at me, one side of his mouth a little crooked. "You are not a follower of Allah?"

"I have no problem with Allah, but no."

"I do not shake hands with infidels. You have cash on you, right now?"

"I do."

He picks up the phone and I hear the young man outside talking with him. He nods, seeming satisfied.

"You came alone?" he asks.

"I have a driver who's also an interpreter."

"You came from Asunsion?"

"We did."

He reaches under his desk and I hear a buzzer ring three times in the outer office, then I hear a door open, but it appears to be the outer door, not the inner, and I hear Alex squeak, "Señor…señor." Then the inner door opens and two of the bearded who were around the table outside—baldy and curly—storm in.

And it doesn't look like they're coming to serve tea.

Chapter Twenty Six

I stand in time to sideslip the butt of an AK aimed at my nose—it does scrape across a cheek—drop to one hand, and side kick the guy in the knee. It folds and he goes down, falling against the second guy, but is between me and the second attacker.

The coat rack is within reach. I grab it and drive it into the face of the second asshole as he's trying to bring the AK up to bear on my gut, then I leap the guy who's on the floor, flopping around like a fish out of water. Twice more I drive the hooks of the coat rack into the guy's wide face. It's gushing blood from gashes from the metal hangars, as he goes back against the wall.

Dropping the rack, I close on him, grab the AK, and fall back, dragging him as he clings as tightly to the weapon as I hoped he would. I drop to my back with both feet in his gut. He goes over my head and releases the AK as he does, and I come up with it in hand and spin to see the fat man with an old Army Colt .45 leveled at my belly. But I have the AK leveled at his.

"You can put one .45 in my gut while I'm cutting you in half with this AK," I snap.

His eyes are flashing fire, but he's standing solid.

"Now, I'm going to back out of here, and we're not going to kill each other," I say, slowly, as I back toward the door and out it and pull it closed behind. "Don't come out of this door," I yell, but have stepped aside, if he fires through the door, I'm out of the line of fire.

He doesn't fire, and I head for the outer door just as it opens and the other two bearded guys come charging in. I meet the first one with the butt of the AK and he goes down like the bag of shit I'm sure he is. I meet the other one as he's trying to swing the muzzle of his weapon to me. I catch it with one hand on the barrel, get a half step closer, and bury a knee in his crotch, then drive the banana clip of the AK I'm carrying in one hand into his throat. He suddenly loses interest in those seventy-two virgins he's been promised and hits the ground, clasping his personals with both hands.

I think I'm home free, but then the door between the offices bursts open and the guy I'd flipped over exits in a run, sees me, and his muzzle is coming up, but not quickly enough. I fire a three shot burst, blowing him back into the office.

Spinning toward the door, I see Alex running for the outside, but before he gets there the outside guard fills the doorway and he, too, is raising his muzzle. I have no choice, and stitch him with another three shot burst from the AK, and he's flung back outside to the ground.

Fuck, it's a total cluster-fuck. I head back to the office door and clean up my mess by emptying the clip into the last standing guy, then into the fat man's desk, which he's kneeling behind and firing the .45 as fast as he can pull the trigger, but only blowing holes in his ceiling. The weapon does kick like hell and is hard to keep down on the target…however, he'll never have to worry about it again.

His .45 rests on the desk, and since they absconded with my Ruger, I help myself to it.

It seems Allah will be busy providing the faithful with virgins. I've often wondered what the virgins think of this arrangement, but Muslims don't seem to consider their feelings.

Alex is screaming and heading out the outside door, then spins on a heel with a move that would make a ballerina jealous and as quickly is screaming and heading back inside. I pass him and get to the doorway in time to see Skip heading my way at a run, and look past him to see the gate guard flat on his back, unmoving.

I yell at him, "Back the cab in. I'll get the doors open."

I only have to push one of the two rolling doors aside, and almost as soon as I get it open, Skip fills it with the cab and backs all the way through it and up to a stack of wooden cases. Alex stands, wringing his hands as we bust open a crate, remove the plastic case, open it, and stuff an RPG in his trunk. As I'm getting it settled, Skip is using his K-Bar to open a case of rocket-propelled grenades and throws a half dozen into the trunk.

I spot a rifle-size case, and I'm pleased to discover a dozen XM-15 Bushmasters, and throw five of them into the trunk, then two cases of five hundred .223's. We leap into the cab, with me driving and Alex looking very dazed. I spin the wheels but only shoot forward until I'm a hundred feet from the warehouse, then slide to a stop, jump out, pop the trunk, grab the RPG and a grenade, load it up, and put one through the open door of the warehouse.

I should have tried the shot from the gate, over a hundred yards from the open door, as the son-of-a-bitch blows so hard it takes me off my feet and I land five feet back on my butt, my hair and eyelashes singed and me gasping for breath. I don't stay there long. I throw the weapon back into the trunk and haul ass through the open gates.

The gate guard is trying to sit up, but looks so groggy that I don't think he'd recognize his mother if she was in his face calling him to supper.

I yell to Skip, "What did you hit him with?"

"My fist." He shakes the left one at me. "This one will put you in the hospital." Then he shakes the other, "and this one will send you to Valhalla…hell, I'm afraid of it myself." I know from experience that he's right.

We fishtail out of there to the sound of lots of explosives lighting the morning behind us. In the rear view mirror I see streaks and contrails filling the sky, and the billowing smoke of high explosives. We leave to the bone-jarring beat of a hard metal band's base, but it's the thud of explosives, not a drum.

By the time we're a mile down the road, we're giving way to passing fire trucks and police and military vehicles, red lights and sirens filling the air.

By noon we're well on our way back to Asuncion, with no one on our tail. It'll be a long time before that scene cools enough that some smart forensics guy discovers that the bodies in the explosion are full of bullet holes…unless, of course, the gate guard has his wits about him. I can only hope that he wants nothing to do with authorities, and that as soon as his head cleared from Skip's pounding, he beat feet for the nearest cover, far away from any police.

Speaking of forensics, I'm eager to find out just exactly what the bite of a banana spider looks like.

It's mid-afternoon, and we're still on the road, this time in the light enjoying the variety of crops and well tended fields as we cross a great fertile plain. My phone goes off with *Ring of Fire* and I know it's Pax.

"What's up?" I answer.

"My adrenalin," he says, then asks, "is everything going your way?"

"So far I'm out of the *jusgados, amigo*."

"You're getting into that *Español*?"

"I just had to brush up on my Arabic, but my teachers all quit on me."

"Some of those names I gave you?"

"Yeah, some of those names. You forgot to tell me they were related to Ali Baba and the forty thieves."

"They try to stick it to you?"

"Actually they tried to stick me up, take the money, and keep the goods."

"Oops, sounds bad…and I'm talking to you on the phone so that means they are no longer talking?"

"Enjoying their time with the virgins, I imagine."

"Enough. You can catch me up over some pasta at Peiros when you get back. And the purpose of your visit?"

"Tonight, or tomorrow night, God willin' and the creek don't rise. So, why is your adrenaline up?"

Chapter Twenty Seven

"That Trojan Horse I put in Wedgeworth's computer...the prick's a kink, more porn than the Vegas strip."

"The hell you say...not old gee whiz golly gee Wedgeworth?"

"One and the same. He has a hideout hard-drive on his computer. I almost missed it. And the worst of it, lots of very, very young girls. And the wife's not a lot better."

"How so?"

"She's been in rehab twice and arrested for DUI a couple of times. A couple of thousand-an-hour Santa Barbara slickers got her off, but she was guilty as hell. One of those times she had all three kids in the car."

"Either he's driving her to drink or she's a dead drunk in the sack. Copy it all somewhere. He's a deadbeat som'bitch and I may need some leverage to get paid if we get the hell out of here."

"No if's, *amigo*. It's *when*. I don't want to have to come down there and save your ass. Anything I can do for you here?"

"I thought I was going to have to have you hit Wedgeworth up for some more front money, but it seems I got my most expensive items for free."

"Again, I'll look forward to hearing the story."

"This is only about halfway through, odds are. Let's hope for a happy ending."

"Be safe."

He hangs up and I guess it's time for me to face up to my most unpleasant task, so I dial the school where Penny Bartlett works, hand the phone to Skip and ask him to ask to speak to the principal. I presume Penny's answering the phones and I don't want her to recognize my voice before I talk to someone who can stand beside her while I give her the worst possible news. Skip gets the principal on line, then hands me the phone.

"Ma'am, you're Penny's boss."

"Yes, who is this?"

"I'm a friend of Penny's and I have the worst possible news about her husband. Can you stand close and lend her a shoulder while I break the news to her?"

She's silent for a moment then sighs deeply. "I can. You want me to ask her to pick up this line?"

"I do."

Telling a young woman her husband is dead in another country, or in the next room, is not an easy task, and to be truthful it's all I can do not to sob when I hear her break down. I console her as best I can, then ask her to hand the phone back to her boss and instruct her as to how to call the American embassy and the State Department. Hopefully, they'll get some kind of closure. I know Penny's in for a rough time, as there's been no official report of Toby's death, and there'll be lots of beating around the bushes before anything is settled.

As soon as I hang up, my phone buzzes again. "*Ola*," I say, and am pleased to hear Carmen's voice, but not pleased that she sounds very worried.

"General Maldonado has asked my father to bring me to see him. It seems he's not happy that I entered the country with someone suspected of violating his space."

"Deny, deny, deny," I say.

"Just so you know, I'm breaking off the engagement," she says, then laughs, albeit a little nervously.

"I understand completely," I say, "I'm distraught, but understand."

"I will call you late today and report in."

"Please do."

I hang up, then call Hank Hausman. "Handy man Housman, the repairman's best back-up," he answers.

"You guys manage to stay out of jail?" I ask.

"Yeah, must be jet lag," he says.

"We'll be coming in the back door of the hotel and sneaking up the service elevator if possible. We'll need a little shut eye as it's been a long hot night and an even hotter morning."

"We're standing by," he says, and I hang up.

Alex has had time to come to his senses, and gets his back up as we near town. "So, señor, you think two million is enough?"

"I was going to mention that, Alex. I was thinking another two million for us damn near getting you ventilated—"

"Ventilated?"

"Shot. Another two million, but only if you stick with us for another day or so. Then it's a two million bonus for today, and another four million for tomorrow."

He's quiet for a long time, then shrugs. "So, no more shooting. No more giant bangs…how you say, explosions?"

"God no, *amigo*. This was a very unusual day. That's the bad news. The good news is you did your country a solid—"

"A solid?"

"A very good turn—"

"Good turn?"

"You did a very patriotic thing, helping to get rid of some very bad people who were smuggling dope and weapons to the many rebels in the mountains." And I think he buys it.

Again, he's silent for a long while, then shrugs. "Okay. *Uno mas*...one more day."

We've been very lucky—gringo interlopers in a country where half the law is hunting us. If we can make it one more day we'll be more than merely lucky, it will be serendipity.

Now to sneak into one of the city's largest hotels, and do so without attracting attention and having the law called.

We find a service door, and I'm happy to enter as an employee. We go straight into a dressing room where a dozen waiter uniforms hang in a segmented but open closet, each with a name placard on the shelf above. For the time it takes to get five stories up to the room where Hank, Wetback, and Madman are housed, I'm Emilio and Skip is Skip, because none of the uniforms are big enough to fit the Viking. And my pants look like high-waters on the way, at least two inches above shoe line. Instead of a waiter's rags, Skip finds a tool bag and carries it as if I'm escorting a repairman to a room.

And it works.

Both of us are sawing logs in a few minutes and sleep for a couple of good solid hours before I'm awakened by my phone buzzing.

And it's Carmen.

"I would be in prison were it not for my family," she says.

"I'm sorry. We'll get you out of here and headed back to the states if you want to risk leaving with us."

"I will consider it. So far, I'm fine. Screamed at in front of my uncle and father by that pig Colonel Vargas, but I've been screamed at before. I survived. However, if you try to go back on the airport, you may not."

"Why's that?"

"General Maldonado and the pig Vargas have enlisted the help of the Pyragüés. They are now guarding the Air Force hangars."

"And you said these were very, very bad boys."

"The worst. Killers and rapers of women and children, torturers of the innocent…in the most terrible ways you can imagine. Thousands were murdered when Stroessner was in power. They no longer go by that name, not since Stroessner was deposed, but it's the same scum of the earth. I wish they were all dead and rotting in hell."

"Thanks for the heads up," I say, then lie, "but I have no intention of going to the airport."

"Oh. This is about the new airplane, is it not?"

"What airplane?" I say with such conviction I should be up for an Academy Award.

"*Si*, what airplane. Call me if you need anything, and by the way, you owe me a week's two thousand."

"And I'm dying to pay you."

"And I hope you do before you die." She's being amusing, but then sounds sorry for saying it and adds, "That's a terrible thought. Please be careful."

"Yes, ma'am. I'll call you later."

"Please."

I hang up and we call room service and have a team meeting while we're waiting for a spread...one I hope is not our last meal. Pyragüés or no Pyragüés, we're going after the G5 tonight.

Chapter Twenty Eight

We wait until ten PM, then head out of the hotel. And, of course, I have to act like a total a-hole to keep these guys from sucking down the booze. I have no way of knowing if the G5 is hangared, or is delivering some fat cats to Rio de Janeiro or Buenos Aries. So we must merely take our chances.

The plan is for Madman and Skip to head for the fuel dump and handcuff the attendant or attendants, to something permanent, wait thirty minutes, then drive the jet fuel truck to the hangar. Skip has one of the handhelds, so we're in touch. Hank and I will take the guards out, hopefully in relative silence, keeping Wetback out of harm's way if possible. We're presuming there are only two guards at the hangar. Then we'll set up a perimeter to keep any other Pyragüés gentlemen at a distance if they become aware of our presence, all while Wetback is preflighting the plane. We stand guard, while Skip and Madman fuel the plane, if need be, and then tractor it out of the hangar.

I'm counting on the guards being very hesitant to fire on the G5, as it's the general and colonel's pride and joy.

Then we load up, and wing our way to the good old US of A.

Simple, right?

Wrong.

Nothing goes as planned and I'm sure Murphy's law applies in South America just as it does in North.

Again there are too many of us for one cab, so Alex has to call on his cousin. I part with another million guarani. Both Alex and Alfredo seem very happy to be cut loose, and I'm sure break a codebook full of traffic laws on their way back to town.

I'm toting the RPG; Hank, after a few lessons, is my loader and will carry the grenades until we stow them behind the hangar and move to take out the guards. Wetback will guard the stash, and hopefully stay out of the action until it's time to do his trick in the right seat of the G5.

To my surprise, the cut in the fence is still open, apparently undiscovered, even though the rag is still flapping in the breeze.

The rest of them remain outside the fence in the cover of the brush while I repeat my trick with the whistle, the steaks, and the sleeping pills. This time the dogs seem almost glad to see me, and consume the steaks as if it's their normal feeding. I dismount from the tower as soon as they close their eyes. I give the boys a call on the hand-held and they jog my way. Skip carries the RPG as far as the tower, then he and Madman head for the fuel dump. Although it's a fairly dangerous mission as the fuel dump is well lit, I think it propitious to keep the pilots apart. If one of them takes a round, the other can still fly us out.

We've all sworn to one mission plan, and that's to get the aircraft in the air, no matter if one or more of us has to remain behind. If we have a pocketful of money when the mission's complete, we each swear to return to Paraguay and spring whoever might be captured, or die trying. It's a blood oath, and I trust each of these guys to fulfill it if necessary.

I'm happy to note that no new surveillance cameras seem to be mounted at the rear of the G5 hangar. We're all dressed in black, as are the guards, so I'm hoping that even if spotted, we'll be mistaken for one of their own.

Hank takes the east side of the hangar and I the west, checking our watches as we set out, agreeing to give ourselves one minute to get the drop on the guards.

I hadn't noticed before, as I was fairly busy hotfooting it away from the hangar, but the areas to the sides and rear of the hangar are gravel. Damn if I don't sound as quiet as a herd of buffalo as I cover the two hundred feet to the front. Twenty feet before I get there, I see the backlit head and shoulders of a guard peer around the corner of the building, and he yells, "*Paco? Que paso?*"

"*Nada*," I yell back and close on him. His weapon is slung over his shoulder, and I notice him looking to the far corner where Hank should be arriving to take out the other guard. The butt of my Bushmaster takes him just under the ear before he can turn back, and he goes to his knees. I whack him again, then realize that another guard is twenty feet away, coming at a dead run and unslinging his Heckler. I have no choice but to stitch him up the middle with a three shot burst. The Bushmaster is equipped with a suppressor, but the low crack can still be heard for two hundred yards.

As the shot Pyragüés withers on the ground, I hear shots from the far side of the hangar, then a big guy in black is running my way. I flop to the ground, prone, using the fallen guard as a shield, until I see that it's Hank.

"Two fucking guards, not one," he yells, "I had to send one to hell." And we head for the doorway.

"Yeah, here too." Then we're inside and, thank God, so's the stolen fifty million dollar G5.

I radio Wetback, and in seconds he joins us and heads for the aircraft, drops the ramp, and is inside while Hank and I set up. Carrying a couple of heavy metal workbenches outside we dump them on their sides for a makeshift defensive firing position, flop down, and Hank waits while I go from guard to guard and relieve them of their radios and weapons. One is still rolling from side to side and another is moaning. I see no reason to finish them off, as even though Carmen has said they're very bad guys, they are no longer a threat.

With the exception of the occasional wheeze from a lung shot guard, it becomes eerily silent.

Then I hear Wetback call from the plane hatchway. "Hey, Reardon, you gotta see this."

I hustle in and he waves me up the gangway. He's smiling like the proverbial Cheshire cat, and pointing. I get all the way inside before I see what he's talking about.

Every seat in the passenger area, save two, is stacked with over a dozen kilo packages of what must be cocaine, and there are sixteen seats in the back and luggage compartments behind the passenger area. I walk back to the head and open it. There must be five hundred pounds of cocaine filling it. Nobody's using the john on the way home. It's no wonder Vargas enlisted the help of the Pyragüés to guard the hangar. He wouldn't want half the Air Force to know what he was up to. A couple of tons of prime cocaine!

"We heading somewhere we can peddle this?" he asks, still grinning.

"We're heading for Miami, and, no, we're not peddling it. We're using it to make friends with American authorities."

"How the fuck....?" He looks a little perplexed.

"What's the fuel situation?" I ask.

"Surprisingly, she's topped off. I'll be ready to haul ass in fifteen minutes."

"Make sure," I say, and head out to return to Hank, who's keeping a lookout.

As soon as I reach the cover of the turned over work tables, my phone buzzes.

"Roger," I answer. And it's Skip.

"Hey, pard, we've secured the fuel truck. Two assholes in all black uniforms are tied up in the shack. You ready for us to head your way?"

"Change of plans. She's topped off. New plan. Is there transportation there other than the fuel truck?"

"Yes, there's a Toyota jeep with no insignia."

"Must belong to the Pyragüés guards. Can you get a key?"

"Keys are in it."

"Good. By the watch, ten minutes. Figure out how to blow that whole fucking fuel dump. I gotta believe it'll be a great diversion."

"What a party," Skip says, and hangs up.

I call Wetback again. "Hey, I'm calling a buddy in Miami who's tight with the DEA. They'll be waiting for you when you land so don't panic. We'll have it handled."

All that was the good news. The bad is that four vehicles are showing their lights at the Air Force headquarters.

And they're heading this way.

Chapter Twenty Nine

I call Skip back, and it takes him almost ten rings to answer, and the vehicles coming this way are closing fast.

"Hey, don't wait," I tell him, "the shit's about to hit the fan over here. Blow it, haul ass this way."

As quickly as I hang up, I unlimber the RPG. By the time we're locked and loaded, the vehicles are only two hundred yards away. There's a personnel carrier leading the way, what looks like a Mercedes limo next, another personnel carrier behind, and a large vehicle that resembles a half-track, but has two sets of double rubber tires on the rear. There's a fifty caliber mounted on an armor protected tripod on its roof, unmanned but a real threat as it's most likely accessible from the inside.

I radio Wetback who's in the cockpit of the G5. "Yeah," he answers.

"Activate the hangar doors and get ready to fire that baby up."

"There's a small plane behind. We'll blow it over."

"Tough titty...it's about to hit the fan out here."

"Roger," he says, and is gone.

I shoulder the RPG, lie down on the vehicle with the 50 cal, and as soon as I judge it to be a hundred yards, send a rocket its way. It hits low just behind the cab, and the big buggy goes four feet in the air and over on its side.

The leading personnel carrier slams on its brakes, the Mercedes plows into it, and the personnel carrier following rear-ends the Mercedes. One shouldn't tailgate.

I don't know if they didn't see the RPG on its flight there, or what, but the damn fools in the Mercedes pile out as if the buggy in the rear had self-destructed. I flip down my night goggles and damned if it doesn't appear that Colonel Vargas and good ol' Charlie Glascock are first out, followed by two armed guards.

Hank is not bashful; his AR begins to bark with a series of three shot bursts. By the time he gets the second off, both armed guards go down, the sky to the west of us lights up, and for the long count of five it's daylight on our end of the airport and a fireball the size of five of the hangar we're in front of billows five hundred feet in the air.

I have to turn aside, as even at the distance of something over three eighths of a mile, the heat singes my face. Then the fireball recedes to the size of a five-storey building, but the roar is like a freight train passing fifty feet away.

The lead personnel carrier cranks it hard around and is heading back the way it came. The one following the Mercedes is beginning to burn from the fire consuming the half-track. I see Glascock on the ground, crawling away from the burning vehicles, and Vargas crawling back inside. The first vehicle stops after only fifty yards and four guys unload and are beginning to get what's happening, as are the black clad Pyragüés who've exited the one beginning to burn. We're seeing muzzle flashes and hearing the buzz of bullets and pings as they hit the hangar and the steel work tables we're behind.

"Reload!" I yell at Hank, and he does so. This time I roll to the side and the next rocket propelled grenade takes the Mercedes in its side. It, too, blows and flips over, it's bottom facing us.

I can see another set of headlights coming our way, the vehicle bounding over some rough terrain. And I can hear the huge hangar doors behind me beginning to grind open.

Lets hope these guys have some respect for the fifty million dollar G5, as I doubt if she'll get far full of bullet holes.

Hank is firing and empties his first clip, and doing a hell of a job as the guys who piled out of the burning personnel carrier have quit firing, obviously out of the fight. The ones in the leading vehicle, who stopped some hundred and fifty yards from us, are well covered and firing from behind that lightly armored wagon.

I presume the vehicle bouncing our way is Skip and Madman, and then am assured of it as it swings behind the vehicle from which we're still taking fire. Those guys probably think it's their buddies coming to help, and they get a big surprise as muzzle flashes erupt from that Toyota, raking the four guards hiding there. Then Skip hits the throttle hard and comes our way.

The hangar doors are open and Skip flies past us and slides the Toyota under the wing of the G5, and he and Madman leap out. Skip heads up the gangway into the plane, but Madman comes our way and drops down behind the tables, joining us.

"Good job blowing the fuel dump," I yell at him, over the roar of the G5 engines.

"Damn near turned us ass-end over teakettle as we were heading out. Fuck, what a fireball! The fourth of fucking July," he says, a slightly awestruck grin on his face. He's carrying an AR and some fire begins coming from the distant personnel carrier again, plinging on the hangar behind and on the steel table.

"Guess we missed one," he says.

"Ka ka happens, " I offer, then yell to Hank to load me up again, and it's a good thing I do as there are three more vehicles leaving the headquarters area, and they're not in retreat. They're headed our way.

For the first time, as he comes to load, I see Hank has blood covering his shoulder and right chest.

"You're hit," I say, and he glances down.

"Damned if I'm not."

"Get your ass in the plane," I snap.

"I can still fight."

"Get your ass in the plane," I yell.

"I'll stay with Mike," Madman says. "Wetback can fly if something happens to me."

I shove Hank toward the plane, and he drops his AR and clips, leaving them with us, stays low, and crabs the fifty or sixty feet to the ramp.

I can feel my radio vibrate, and put it to my ear. It's Wetback.

"Hey, you fuckers better get aboard. We need to haul ass."

"You'll never make the runway. More bad guys on their way. Haul ass for Miami. We'll catch up."

"How the hell are you gonna do that?"

"You haul ass, that's an order if you want your quarter mil, cause we won't get a dime unless you go."

"You're the man," he says, and I see the gangway begin to rise as the plane engines roar louder and she shudders then begins to creep forward, even while the ramp is closing.

"Pay attention," I say to Madman, and give him a quick lesson in loading the RPG and staying the fuck out of the way when I fire.

Wetback turns sharply away from the oncoming vehicles, now only a quarter mile, and pours it to the G5, which is both good and bad. Good because they're hauling ass toward the main runway and won't have to take fire from the bad guys who are closing fast; bad because the backwash from the engines blows the steel tables sliding away from Madman and me, and blows Madman off his feet; he spins across the tarmac. Dragging the RPG, the remaining two shells, and my AR, I head for the cover of the hangar and scream at him to follow.

By the time we're set up again in the walk-through door of the hangar, the vehicles are only three hundred yards and closing, and the single guard left behind the personnel carrier is finally zeroing in. I decide, since I have one loaded and two grenades left, to take him out, and put an RPG in the side of that carrier. One hundred and fifty yards is a good distance for the grenade, but it hits the carrier low and although it doesn't turn it over on the prick behind, ignites it in a ball of fire, and the shooting stops.

As quick as Madman can load me up, I'm zeroing in on another half track coming our way, and it's a good thing I am, as its 50 cal is lighting the night and stitching the top of the hangar. Thank God the guy on the gun is no good at fifty miles an hour, and I don't have to take cover out of the doorway, not that the light metal of the hangar would do much good. I nail his ass as he reaches about a hundred eighty yards distance, hitting him in the front, and the halftrack careens away crazily. The other three vehicles are personnel carriers, probably with four guys each, but they turn away and hightail it when they see the mother ship on fire and weaving in goofy jerks across a grassy area between taxiways.

I take a quick recon of the hangar and see that the Citabria is stacked up like so much cordwood in a corner, but the Icon seems to be intact. And she's beautiful and flexible, with wheels below floats.

"Can you fly that Icon?" I ask Madman.

"I can fly a fucking barn door, you get me on an edge."

Chapter Thirty

I love pilots. "Check it out. We'll get a lot farther in the Icon than in a fucking Toyota."

And he hauls ass toward the little plane. Luckily, no one has retracted its folding wings, so we don't have to learn our way around that while ducking AK47 or Heckler fire.

I keep watch, sending the occasional burst at the vehicles, now gathering four hundred yards from the hangar.

I'm down to one grenade. And not only are there two vehicles only four hundred yards away, but there are another five leaving the Air Force headquarters, and I doubt if they'll be so easily fooled. They are probably down to regular Air Force guards by now and I really don't want to dust some poor yokel who's just trying to get by in the world.

To my great pleasure, I hear the Icon fire up and it begins taxiing my way.

It stops, still slightly sheltered by the hangar, and the canopy opens and Madman is smiling—like a madman. I run for it, still carrying the RPG and my AR, but he yells at me. "No room for the launcher."

So I trot back to the doorway.

No sense wasting a grenade. Even though the approaching vehicles are still three hundred yards distant, I launch one their way. It'll never reach the target, but it'll give them something to sweat.

I throw the RPG aside and run for the Icon, and before I can get the canopy to close, Madman has the throttle to the firewall and the little hotrod is hauling ass toward the runway.

Just as I think we're clear, I hear him yell, "Jesus Christ," and look over to see his forehead bleeding badly. I look back to see holes in the canopy beside me, then over to see more holes in his side of the cover.

"Put pressure on it," I say.

"You gotta take it," he says, as his eyes are filling with blood.

Thank God the Icon has a stick at both side-by-side seats, although all the instruments are in front of the pilot's left seat.

I take the stick, settle my feet on the pedals, and search my brain for what little I know about flying. I took lessons long enough to land the damn little Cessna 150 I learned in, but then didn't worry about more…for it was just for one of these kinds of emergencies I tried to learn. Get the damn thing down in one piece was my mantra.

Of course you had to learn to get the damn things up before you had to worry about getting one down. I've never flown without an instructor in the left seat, where I now sit, but I guess there's a first time for everything.

The little plane responds nicely to the stick and peddles, and I head down the runway, and it's a good thing I do, as tracers are singing, cutting the air, all around us.

I have no idea what take off speed is so as we reach ninety kilometers on the indicator, I ease the stick back. She literally jumps into the air like the sweet bird she is.

Behind us the fuel dump still blazes and at least two vehicles burn on the tarmac.

Now, if I can just keep Madman alive, and figure out where the hell we're going so we can get him to a hospital.

Then I notice the fuel gauge.

Oops, we have a lousy quarter tank.

And me with fifty jumps and no parachute! Then I remember, the plane has one. Yes, the little Icon has its own emergency parachute, and even though she won't sting like a bee, to quote Ali, she'll float like a butterfly if need-be.

"Get your shirt off and wrap your head," I yell at Madman, but it seems it's all he can do to keep pressure on his forehead, and is using both hands to do so.

We stay that way, with me taking a heading of about one hundred eighty degrees as I know it will quickly take us into Argentina and out of Paraguayan air space—not that I think they won't pursue us to hell and back.

Just as I settle down, take a deep breath, and begin gaining some confidence, a jet roars by so close it rocks the wings of the little plane.

"What was *that*?" Madman asks.

"Big fucking trouble," I say, and look over my shoulder to see another T33 bearing down on us.

They do over 300 knots and we top out at 135 or so.

We're double fucked.

"Turn the radio to 225," Madman instructs, and I do.

"Emergency channel?" I say as I'm dialing, "nobody gives a rat's ass."

"Yeah, but they may be trying to contact us and give us instructions."

In moments the radio crackles with Spanish, and I pick up the mike and reply, "*No comprendo*," and do so while I'm madly looking for a way out.

The two T33's, with the nice little—probably 30 caliber—machine guns mounted under each wing, come alongside, having to throttle way back to slow to our speed.

The radio crackles again and this time it's broken English.

"Turn 180 degrees, back to airport. Or we keel you!"

"*Si*. Will do. You have to get off my wing so I can."

"*Habla despacio*...I no understand."

I've got an idea, but it'll probably get us killed. I've been searching the ground for an opening, somewhere to dump this little beauty in, as we can land in any six hundred foot clearing in the jungle...probably wreck the plane and kill us both with me flying, but the plane is capable of it.

But better yet, I see the moon reflecting off a long stretch of water, undoubtedly the River Paraguay, and either it or a clearing is an escape for us, and the T33's can't land in either. If I can only get down without getting us shot to shit.

We're only at a thousand meters, and I figure we can descend to river level in a little over two minutes without ripping the wings off. The T33's probably can't bank around and get behind us in that short a time.

"I'm going for the river," I tell Madman.

"Altitude?"

"A thousand meters."

"Kill your lights, nose her down steep, and when you get close, turn on only the landing light just long enough to judge your altitude and be ready to kill it if we make it down."

"Will do."

I've been slowly throttling back as we talk—not so slow we'll stall, I pray, but so the T33's think we're trying to turn. They get wise that I can't turn with them on my wing, and both peel off to a hundred yard distance, having to give it the throttle so they don't stall.

I shove the stick forward, hard, and she noses over and we suddenly lose visual of the T33's.

I can hear Madman counting. "One, two, three, four, five, six, seven, eight…now, back on the stick and bring her to about one hundred meters a minute descent. When you figure you're thirty or forty meters over the water, follow my instructions."

"Will do, damn, we're still losing altitude fast."

Chapter Thirty One

"Give her some throttle."

"We're at tree top level."

"Frigging trees are two hundred feet tall, so back off on the throttle until you're ten feet off the water, then you're going to kill the power and flare her in. We may hit hard, and may flip the little fucker, so pop the cowling so we can escape."

I do so and the wind whistles.

"Ease the throttle off and when she begins to settle, flare it back so you've got ten degrees or so, nose up."

"Hang on," I yell as the water seems to be rushing up at us.

The river catches the back of the floats, and we're violently thrown forward, and I think we're going to somersault, but she stands up until our nose is in the water, then she settles, and as she does I hear the roar of the jets passing overhead and see plumes of water from the machine guns not ten feet off our wing.

"You flared too much."

"Fuck you, we're alive."

"Granted. Good job."

"Thanks. The current's taking us," I yell at Madman.

"Can you give her some throttle so you've got some control?"

I do so and head for the right bank as if I'm anywhere near where I think I am, that's Argentina. Then I realize I'm under the overhang of the huge trees that flank River Paraguay for hundreds of miles.

"Hey, we're out of sight under the trees."

"Cool," Madman says. Then offers, "I'm dizzy as hell and may pass out. As this is a water plane there should be a tether line somewhere. Is there anyway you can get us anchored until the friggin' Paraguayan Air Force gives up?"

To the T33 pilots credit they've gone on down river, made a one eighty, and I can see them coming back our way, not fifty feet off the surface and well below the tree tops. Gutty flying to my way of thinking, as the river does curve some. The good news is at that level where I don't think we can be seen, and they damn well have to keep their eyes fixed ahead so they don't eat it in the jungle.

"We still drifting?" Madman asks.

"We are, but it seems safe—"

Before I get the words out, a sagging branch catches a wingtip and we spin. As soon as we make a two seventy I give her some throttle, we ease back out into the main stream, and I get her headed downstream.

"Can you see well enough to keep us out of trouble?" Madman asks.

"Yeah, the moon's ahead of us and lights the river like a runway."

"You got enough room to get us back in the air?"

"Friggin' river is over a half mile wide and I bet I've got five miles of smooth water ahead."

"Then fly me to a friggin' doc before I bleed to death."

Nothing bleeds much worse than a deep scalp wound. His is across the forehead hairline, and nothing but pressure and stitches will stop the gushing. But it usually looks far worse than it really is. There's little question in my mind that he has a concussion, which worries me more than the bleeding.

So I get back to the business at hand. "Okay, how do I get this little beauty off the water?"

"Shove it to the wall. Don't try to lift off the water until you've got at least ninety kilomerters of airspeed, then you're gonna pop her up breaking the suction of the water, then slightly drop the nose, level out, gain airspeed, then climb out."

"Got it, cross your fingers and toes."

It's easier than I might have believed, but I almost put her back in the water when I try to level her off. I don't mention that to my instructor as I get her under control and gaining altitude until we're soon over the treetops. Far behind I see the lights of the two T33's as they sweep back and forth over the river, back about where we originally landed. The tunnel of trees saved our ass. The current carried us most of a mile and our takeoff took us another half mile so I'm crossing my fingers and toes that we're far out of their ability to pick us out. Even then I'm staying just over the tree tops for a while.

I get the strange sensation that I'd liked to have tied the little plane up to the shore, taken a fishing rod out or cut a pole, dug for some worms, and spent about a week on my butt on the bank hoping I didn't catch anything I'd have to clean. But no, I've chosen to be chased by a couple of young wild ass pilots with machine guns on the wings. Of course there is the matter of a two-point-five-million-dollar fee. There is that.

I stay over the tree tops for at least five miles, then begin to slowly ascend to a safer altitude, then aloud, exclaim, "Fuck!"

"What?" Madman asks.

"We got a low fuel indicator light."

"Just what we need," he says, and sighs deeply. "Any lights anywhere?"

"I've got to get a little altitude."

"We don't want to go down in this friggin' jungle," he says.

"No shit, Sherlock," I say, but it doesn't need saying.

When we get back to one thousand meters, I see the dim glow of lights a few miles away to my right, and wing over and head that way. The odds of them having an airstrip are pretty good, but even if they don't, we might be able to survive setting this little beauty down in their main street…if they have a main street.

"Lights ahead," I say.

He merely sighs again. Then mumbles, "I wish I could fucking see, but I'm dizzy as hell."

"The bleeding seems to have slowed."

"Yeah, that's the good news…the bad is I'm flying over the fucking jungle with somebody who's made about five landings on a wide swatch of airport, and there ain't no wide swatch of airport around."

I don't bother to respond. Then I'm over the lights of what appears to be an *estancia* or maybe a mine or timber company headquarters. If there's an airstrip, I sure as hell don't see it, but they wouldn't have it lit unless they were expecting a plane. I see Madman fumbling for the radio mike, then get it to his lips. "Mayday, mayday. Anyone on the radio?"

Silence as I circle.

"Mayday," he says again, and to my surprise a voice comes back.

"*Si, señor. Problema?*"

"Yeah, we got a problem. We're out of fuel. Can you get some lights on your strip?"

"You English?"

"American."

"You got helicopter?"

"No, airplane."

"We got no strip, only helicopter pad."

"Fuck."

"Señor, we is a Catholic facility."

"Sorry. We're turning our lights on so you'll know where we're gonna crash."

"We will watch, señor."

He turns to me. "Any sign of any kind of clearing?"

"I'm gonna parachute—"

"You've got a fucking parachute. Only one I guess?"

Chapter Thirty Two

Even under the circumstances, I have to laugh. "Madman, the *airplane* has a parachute. An emergency chute. I'm taking her up," and just as I get it out, the engine coughs, and I doubt if I'm taking her any higher than she already is. I check the altimeter. "We've got nine hundred meters...is that enough?"

"How the fuck should I know? My F16 didn't have a chute, it had an ejection seat."

"Guess, and tell me what to do."

"It doesn't matter what I think, it is what it is. You got the chute release control?"

"It's a lever overhead between the seats."

"Make sure it's operable, then cut the throttle."

I don't have to, as it plane runs completely out of fuel and suddenly there's a very ominous dead silence...and I hope the "dead" part is not foretelling.

"Okay," he says, thinking I cut the engine. "Ease the stick back and just as she shudders about to stall, as slow as you're gonna get, pop the chute."

"Remind me never to get in a fucking airplane again," I say, as the plane slows and I do as instructed, easing the stick back.

"You probably won't have to worry about making that decision," he says, as the stall warning light flares on the control panel and the warning buzzer goes off like a cheap alarm clock.

"Yeah, probably," I concur, loud enough to be heard over the angry buzzing.

The plane starts to nose over and I pull the lever, having no idea what's going to happen, as we begin to accelerate toward the ground.

I hear a swooshing noise, the flapping of fabric, then feel a violent jerk and we're suddenly fairly level again, but swinging as if on a pendulum.

"Crocodiles," Madman says.

"Crocodiles?" I ask.

"Yeah, fucking crocs, or pythons, or man eating fucking jaguars, or some fucking thing has to be waiting for us, the way it's been going."

"You're a glass half empty kind of guy, aren't you?"

"I'm a fucking realist."

"We're still descending at three hundred meters a minute." Fuck, I said she'd float like a butterfly, but she's falling a little like a rock.

"Crap," Madman says, then adds, "I hope what's waiting is a soft landing. That's too fast."

"I hope what's waiting for us is a bottle of Jack Daniels—"

"The blood of Christ."

"Pardon me?"

"The sacrament is probably the only booze they have at some Catholic facility."

"That'll do," I say, and then something crashes, banging my head hard on the windscreen, and suddenly we're upside down hanging on our seatbelts, bouncing back and forth like we're the pin ball in an arcade machine. Then we jerk so hard I about lose my molars and the seatbelt bites deep into my gut.

We're canted at a forty five degree angle, nose down, with the seats still under us, but at least we've stopped.

"We're alive," Madman says, with a little astonishment.

There's a small bug-out bag behind the seats, and I dig into it and come up with a flashlight. I push the canopy up and shine it out to see we're obviously in a tree with the chute entangled in the branches above. Hallelujah. And we seem to be fixed in place. Then I shine it down, and to my dismay, the light diminishes before ground appears. I have no friggin' idea how high we are in this bloody tree. The trunk is only ten feet to my right, and appears to be about two feet in diameter. I know that many of these big jungle beauties, and there are millions of acres of them, are as big as four feet at the base, so we could be a hundred feet in the air...ten friggin' stories.

"Don't step out for a smoke," I suggest.

"Long first step?" he asks.

"Longer than the beam of the flashlight."

"I guess we wait for morning."

"I have to get to a phone."

"Try your cell."

I laugh. "It isn't that big a facility."

"Now who's a half empty glass kind of guy?"

To my great surprise, I get a signal and in moments am talking with a bail bondsman buddy, Fast Freddy Franklin, who I've worked for in Florida a couple of times. He's happy to make some points with the DEA, for whom his brother-in-law, Irish Jack O'brien works, by informing them that the repairman and friends are delivering a couple of tons of grade A cocaine to them via a beautiful G5, and in a few hours they'll be making a soft touchdown and welcoming them aboard. I spent many an hour with Freddy chasing down a couple of skips, and even broke bread with his brother-in-law a couple of times. A good guy, for a fed.

Now if only Wetback and Skip don't decide to fly away to some profitable locale and become multimillionaires comfortable on some island retreat. But I know Skip wouldn't do that.

My second call is to Carmen. She must have been sitting on the phone as she answers before the first ring's complete. "*Ola*," she says, and sounds anxious.

"*Ola, señorita.*"

"Are you okay? The news channel and the internet are buzzing about a raid on our Air Force headquarters—"

"Attributed to whom?" I ask.

"So far it's *Sendero Luminosos,* or Shining Path...no mention of a bunch of gringos."

"Any mention of a couple of tons of cocaine?"

"Cocaine...at the Air Force headquarters?"

"Yes, a couple of tons."

She's silent for a long moment, then her voice sounds with even more concern. "Please tell me you're not here to steal or smuggle cocaine?"

"Carmen, I hate dope, I hate what it does to our country and to yours, and others."

"And you were not here for the airplane, remember what you told me?"

"I do, and I lied, for your own good. We were very surprised to find it loaded with dope, which is on its way to our Drug Enforcement Agency."

She's quiet for another long moment. "Many were killed at the airport."

"I hope many Pyragüés, and I hope they were as bad as you said they were."

"No one has admitted to Pyragüés being there."

"We shot at no one with an Air Force uniform."

"Aw, so Colonel Vargas, who is now dead, a hero so it was said as he rushed to protect his men, was not wearing a uniform?"

"Okay, you got me, but we knew it was him, and he was rushing to protect his dope, not his men."

"Anyone else mentioned in the news?"

"The American pilot was killed."

It's all I can do not to say 'not a bad night's work', but I don't.

"It's over now, Carmen. And I haven't forgotten I owe you money."

"I have an American bank account. I'll send you the wire information."

"Please, but also please call me when you get to the states."

"I'll think about it. *Adios*."

It seems we may not have to wait for daylight as only seconds after I hang up, a powerful torch is sweeping through the canopy near us and finally settles on the fuselage.

We are found. Now we can only hope we're found by friendlies.

The canopy is still loose and I hear someone shout, "Ahoy, the plane!"

And yell back. "Ahoy yourself. We're in one piece."

"Young Jesus climbs like a howler and is on his way with a rope. I'm Father Ailen O'Brian, at your service, me lad. Where in the world did you find a bloody aeroplane with it's own parachute?"

"We'll wait right here, father," I shout back, figuring he can wait to get his questions answered over a tall cold one. I'm encouraged. He may not have a bottle of Jack Daniels, but I'll bet a dime to a doughnut he's got a bottle of Bushmill's or Jameson stashed somewhere.

Chapter Thirty Three

As fate would have it, we dropped into the jungle only a quarter mile from Solange del Argentina Norte, a Catholic orphanage not two miles from a copper mining community with over a thousand employees, which is why we had phone service.

Thanks to a very athletic young man who climbed the hundred feet to bring us a quarter inch line, and to the Priest who waited below with the half-inch line which we pulled up with the first. I was able to do a makeshift loop around the tree with a couple of loops of the lighter line and tie a cask hitch around Madman. We gave a whistle and he was slowly lowered to the jungle floor. The rope returned, and I followed close behind.

Father Ailen is a rosy cheeked gentleman in work clothes and, begorrah, I wasn't wrong—he had a highly valued bottle of Jameson locked away as if it were the Stone of Accord itself, aand he willingly shared it. He also seemed highly skilled in the medical arts, and shared a spool of catgut and did a journeyman's job of stitching Madman's head wound. To Madman's great distress, the father did not allow him to sleep until late the next day, dutifully keeping him awake as he feared the extent of his probable concussion. His wound was easily explained away due to the plane crash, until the morning news of a raid on the Paraguayan Air Force base and the theft of both a G5 and a small Icon. Unfortunately, the father asked what kind of plane it was, and who can lie to a priest?

The good news, he had no love lost for Paraguayans in general and even less for the Pyragües...which he soon learned were the bad guys in the soap opera I played out for him.

It took two days for the father to declare Madman well enough to travel.

As it happened, the weekly supply helicopter from Salta, a northern Argentine city, was propitiously due two days following us dropping in on the good father, his two nun helpmates, and his two hundred charges, mostly Guarani native children. For a slight fee the chopper pilot would let us ride along on its return flight. Then we'd fly commercial—Salta to Buenos Aries, then Miami.

As soon as it was timely, I called Skip to check on their progress, and to my surprise a female voice answered his cellphone.

"Who's calling?" she asked.

"Mike Reardon. Is Skip available?"

Then she worries me. "What relationship do you have to Mr. Allen?"

"We're associates. May I ask who you might be?"

"Agent Alice Zorn, Drug Enforcement Agency."

"So, the airplane and the drugs got there safely?"

"They did. And are you returning to the states? We need a statement from you."

"I'll bet. Yes, I'm coming commercial. Hopefully, if we can get a seat, I'll arrive late tomorrow night or day after tomorrow...as quick as I can."

"Why don't you give me a call when you know your flight and we'll arrange to have you picked up at the airport."

"And welcome me home with a set of iron bracelets? Where's Irish Jack?"

"Who?"

"DEA Agent Jack O'Brian."

"He's in the field."

"I'll hold while you give him a call, or give me his number if you prefer."

"You hold on, I'll see if I can raise him."

In moments she's back on the line and gives me Jack's number. He offers to pick us up and assures me I'll be welcome with open arms, not iron cuffs. He also informs me that Skip, Wetback and Hank are being held "until things get cleared up." Skip is shackled to a hospital bed with what's reported to be a slight wound, but he's always loved the happy juice way too much and as long as they're keeping him shot up, he's happy.

I am being well schooled in the art of soccer while I'm in residence, as the older children of Solange, which I learned meant angel of the sun, engage in the sport almost every waking hour when not doing their chores.

These folks are doing good work, and I put them on my list of benefactors from the proceeds of my trip to South America, should I in fact collect the fee due.

In less than seventy two hours from making the call to Irish Jack, we deplane to find him at the end of the jetway. Standing next to him is a stately redhead, whose lithe appearance is only marred by the lump of a pistol and holster on her waist, her manly haircut, and a snarl a pit bull would envy. Although we are not cuffed, she trails behind, a hand balanced on the butt of her pistol, as Irish Jack leads us to the luggage carousel and then out to a double-parked big black Ford Expedition. In another half hour Madman and I are in separate interrogation rooms at the Miami DEA office.

My instructions to Madman are simple: we were fired on by Paraguayan bandits and dope smugglers while repossessing a G5, which we were contracted to recover.

Irish Jack's boss is a black dude who must have played tackle for the Chargers. Al Washington has a smile that lights the room, and seems a little bemused at the fact that we've delivered him a couple of tons of high quality snort. He plays good cop, and Miss Zorn continues the snarl and plays bad, doing an excellent job.

They grill me for three hours until I can hardly hold my eyes open and keep yawning. Then two State Department types, Frick and Frack, show up and sit in for another hour, but as they've had no official complaint from the Paraguayan government, only a call from our embassy, they're merely observers. Finally, to my great surprise, they cut me loose after confiscating my passport so I won't leave the country...as if that would keep me from doing so if I wanted to.

They do tell me not to leave Miami, and I smile and nod. After we spring Skip from the hospital much to the chagrin of the nurses, the five of us are on a flight to LAX one hour after walking out of the DEA office, after telling them we're heading for a good old American hamburger joint.

It's four PM when we touch down at LAX, and I'm thrilled to note that no armed individuals are awaiting us at the end of that jetway.

What is awaiting is a call from my young friend Athena Wedgewood, Tenee to her friends. My phone says she called at three twenty, only an hour before we walked out of the terminal into the California sunshine, so I return her call.

"You called back," she answers.

"Hi, kid. Of course I called back."

"Can you go to work for me now?"

"Not quite. I have to conclude my business with your father first."

"I'm going to kill him."

That makes me catch a breath. "Hold on now, kiddo. That's crazy talk."

"Are you somewhere I can send you a very private picture?"

"Of course."

"Call me back when you get it."

"You bet. Hey, kiddo, don't do anything stupid."

"Call me back."

"Will do."

While we're loading the limo to Avis with duffle bags, my iPhone vibrates with an incoming email, and as I climb in the cab I open the attachment...and my jaw clamps hard enough that I might fracture my molars.

A fairly good shot of what appears to be Athena Wedgeworth, leaning over her father, who's prone on a bed, her preforming fellatio, or more commonly, a blow job.

"Mother fucker," I say aloud, and both Skip and Madman, who are closest to me in the limo, turn and eye me.

"What's up?" Skip asks.

"My adrenaline," I say, then add, "I'll fill you in after I have a chat with Wedgeworth." Skip might summarily rip the guys head off, and I don't want that to happen until after I collect. But maybe just after.

The boys have all decided to stick with me; I guess it's something about the quarter million each of them has coming.

As I'm waiting for Skip to handle the rental of two cars, and after my adrenaline has calmed a little, I return Tenee's call.

"That appears to be you and your father," I say.

"It is. My sis was hiding in the closet and took the picture. He'd kill us if he knew we had it. Now do you see why I'm going to kill him?"

"Tenee, don't do anything until I get there. I'll be at your house tonight. Don't tell anyone, and I mean anyone, not even your sister, that you showed me that terrible picture, or that I'm on my way."

She's silent so I add, "Agreed?"

"Are you going to kill him for me?" she asks.

"I'll make him wish he were dead, and he'll never bother you again."

"Or my sister?"

"Or your sister. You stay out of his way until I get there."

"Okay, I will."

Now, if I can just keep from killing the worthless prick.

Chapter Thirty Four

It takes us three hours with the terrible traffic, and is seven PM when we pull up to Lucky's. I ask Hank, Madman and Wetback to get a fat steak and a few drinks while Skip and I take care of business. I've still not told any of them about the photo which is residing in my iPhone, and which I've sent to Pax for safekeeping.

Skip will go with me, as there will be some no-necks guarding the Wedgeworth estate.

We make a simple plan. I drop him off out of sight of the guardhouse and move up and stop even with the little passthrough. It's the same gym rat who was at the gate the first time I came.

"Having to work nights now?" I ask.

"May I ask your business?" he asks, as officious as ever.

"I'm Mike Reardon, here to see Mr. Wedgeworth."

He eyes a clipboard, then looks up. "You're not on my schedule."

"Call him."

"That's not how it's done here. I don't bother the house unless it's an emergency."

"Look at me, sunshine. I'm your emergency, so call him."

"You should make the turn around and leave now."

I shrug, then dial Wedgeworth on the throwaway phone I left him. I'm not surprised when he doesn't answer.

Gym rat is patiently waiting, and when I pocket the phone, says, "You must make the turn around, and leave, otherwise I'll have to presume you have some malicious intent, and will call the sheriff and, while the cops are coming, I'll physically throw you off the property and I'll really, really enjoy doing so." He gets a tight grin then picks up the phone.

Skip is alongside the guardhouse, and I give him a nod. The Viking storms the castle with a smashing kick to the door that damn near takes it off its hinges, and in two steps puts one alongside the guard's head, knocking him out from under his Wedgeworth embroidered bill cap. Then as the guy bounces off the wall, uses his own momentum to throw him through the door out prone into a patch of ivy. He's right behind the guy, and as gym rat tries to sit up, grabs him by the tie with his left and smashes two hard rights into his nose, which was broken with the first one. He relieves the guy of his sidearm, then steps back into the guardhouse, looks around, then nods to me as he hits a button and the gates begin to swing aside.

As agreed, he stays at the guardhouse while I go on alone, winding my way up the long driveway.

Like an apparition, Tenee steps out of the sandpaper oaks. I brake and lower the window.

"It is you," she says, as she comes over and leans on the door.

"As promised."

"You will kill him for me?" she asks.

"I didn't say that, Tenee. I will, however, as I did say, make him wish he were dead."

"Can I come up with you? He's still in his office."

"No, you may not. Please wait in your room. Someone will come for you. You won't have to spend another night in the same house with him."

"Go up and take care of your little brother and sister."

"Okay, but only for an hour. Then I'm out of here. I...I can't stay here anymore...."

"It won't take an hour."

She fades back into the copse of trees, and I idle on up the driveway.

I'm not surprised to see another gym rat stationed outside the eight-car garage. He's seated in a lounge chair, reading. I presume he's somewhat blinded by the bright reading light he has clamped to the arm of the chair. As it's not yet dark, I don't have my lights on and he doesn't look up until I'm only a hundred feet or so from him. Then he jumps up as if he's been hit with a cattle prod.

I roll another fifty feet his way as he's madly studying his clipboard, then I roll to a stop and climb out.

"How did you get in?" he asks as I stride his way.

I shrug. "Mr. Wedgeworth called the gate," I lie.

"Wrong. He always calls me if there's an unexpected visitor." He reaches for a radio clipped to his belt, and not for the semi-auto on his other side.

I'm closing the distance as he fumbles with it, and as he raises it to his mouth, put a lot behind a straight right that snaps his head back like he's been rear-ended by a freight train. The radio goes one way, the clip board the other, his head hits the garage door, and he sinks to a sitting position his head slumped onto his chest. He'll be out of my hair for a while, and when he comes to he won't be too eager to find me again. I relieve him of the firearm and stuff it in my belt. A Glock...nice.

I walk into the pass through door and find the pantry door, then the stairway that I know leads directly to Wedgeworth's office.

He's at his broad desk, head down, studying a spreadsheet, as I cross the room. He looks up, and his eyes go salad-plate round, but before I can get to him he hits a button under his desk. In two more steps I have him by the throat with one hand and drag him to his feet, then shove him, maybe a little too violently, back against a bookcase that covers the wall behind him.

Just as I slam him into the bookcase, the door to the outer office opens, and his personal secretary, the Polish beauty Tatya, is silhouetted there.

"Don't hurt him," she says, looking a little confused, and I let him come a foot off the bookcase, then slam him back again hard enough that his eyes roll. Then I drag him over and shove him back into his seat.

He sits there gasping for breath as I haul the phone out of my pocket, bring up the picture, and drop the phone on his desk.

I wave Tatya over and point to the phone. "Did you know that was going on?" I ask. She picks up the phone but stands and stares at him for a moment, the returns it to its cradle as she stares at the screen on the phone.

"God, no," she says with a hand to her mouth, and gives her boss a look like he is the cesspool scum he's proven to be.

"Is Mrs. Wedgeworth home?" I ask, as I flip the phone to Prather K., and he grabs it up and stares in horror, then his expression turns smug. Tatya nods, and I say, "Get her." And she hurries out of the room.

"Photoshop," he says, and curls his lip. I step over and backhand him, splitting the formerly curled upper lip, and he cries out like the little girl he's not allowed his daughter to be.

"Bullshit," I reply. "That's not what Athena told me. Sit there and shut up until your wife gets here."

"What are you going to do?" he asks, and again his look is fearful, as blood trickles out of the corner of his mouth.

"I should rip your fucking deviate head off, but I haven't decided yet. You and your wife and Tatya and I are going to have a little talk, then I'll decide your fate, fuckhead."

In moments Tatya is back, with a very angry Portia Wedgeworth in tow, and she's wavering as if she's spent the afternoon in some cocktail lounge...as usual, I guess.

"Sit down," I instruct them both.

"I was getting ready for my bath," Portia slurs, looking disgusted.

"Sit the fuck down," I say, taking a bit of a threatening step her way, and she quickly sinks into a chair across the desk from her husband. Tatya remains standing, her arms folded, glaring at her boss.

"Show her the picture," I snap at Wedgeworth, who has his face in his hands.

"No," he manages to mumble, so I step closer to the desk, pick the phone up, and toss it into Portia's lap.

She picks it up and as if in disbelief, stares at it, turns it to one side, then the other, then looks at her husband as her face begins to redden. Before I can stop her, she leaps up and dives across the desk, her fingernails, like cougar's claws, rake his face. Stripes of blood surface along both of his cheeks. I grab her around the waist and sit her back in her chair. She tries to rise, but I put both hands on her shoulders, shove her down with authority, and command,

"You stay. Don't move, or I'll see you're in a cell next to that prick."

She's breathing rapidly, like a cheetah that's just run a springbok to ground, her mouth open, her eyes wide, as she glowers at Prather.

"Okay, this is how it's going to be. Prather, you're going to wire two point five million to my account."

Chapter Thirty Five

"The plane's impounded. You didn't do your job," Wedgeworth says, and I'll give him this—he's got balls. Tiny ones, but balls.

"The plane is home in the USA, so yes, I did my job. You'll get it as soon as the DEA sees fit to cut it loose. Now, again, you'll wire two point five million to my account in the Caymans. But that's just the beginning. You'll also pay Hank Hausman every dime you owe him, plus interest at ten percent."

Then I turn to Portia. "And you, ma'am, unless you want your husband to spend many very unproductive years behind bars, will commit yourself to a rehab, and stay until they say your cured of alcoholism—"

"I'm no drunk," she snaps, but slurs even those words.

I reply, slowly but emphatically, "I don't think you can get cured of stupidity, which you're obviously infected with, but they might be able to cure you of alcoholism. So unless you want a change of lifestyle, much for the worse, you'll do exactly like I say."

"Bull crap," she says.

"Exactly. This whole life of yours and Prather's has been bull crap, but the important thing is no matter what else happens…a few years in the graystone mansion if you insist…that picture will be all over the internet if you don't do exactly as I say, and I don't think you want that for your daughter." I threaten, but for Tenee's sake, would never do it.

But this widens Portia's eyes again, then her face is buried in her hands and she begins to sob. Now both of their faces are hidden from view.

I turn back to Prather. "You will move out of this house. Tatya will be paid four times what she's currently making, with a three year firm contract, to stay here and watch over the kids, and you'll both sign to give her temporary custody of the kids until you're proclaimed cured." I step over and put a finger in Prather's chest. "You'll also seek treatment from the best psychiatrist in the land because you're one sick fuck. You'll not see your kids until you, and I, get a green light for visitation from whomever I find to treat you. You'll also have the kids see the best in the land for some psychiatric help, for as long as they need it. But not the same doctor, so there's no chance they'll stumble into your sorry ass."

"That's ridiculous."

I lean down, only two feet from his face. "Let me ask you, fuckface...how good have your bodyguards been?"

He looks a little sheepish, so I answer for him.

"They, and anyone you can hire, can't keep me from putting a bullet in your sick fucking head, and if you don't do exactly what I say, that's your fate. But if the situation is right, first I'll put one in your right knee, then the left, then one in each elbow, then, as should have happened long ago, I'll blow your balls off...and all the fucking money in the world won't keep me from putting you deep six where you fucking well belong. If I didn't have a lot of respect for your daughter, Tenee, you'd be fucking worm food already. Do you understand me?"

He's now looking green. His lip has bled all over his yellow power tie and white shirt.

"He's right," Portia says. "He's absolutely fucking right."

So it's Portia's turn. "And you'll clean up your mouth around your kids," I say, just as an afterthought. Then I turn to Tatya. "Is all this okay with you?"

"How about having him castrated?" she asks, and Prather turns even more green.

"Not a bad idea," I say.

But then she offers, "I love those kids, even though they're all three spoiled rotten, and not from overindulgence by their parents, obviously, but from the lack of parental guidance."

I finally sigh deeply, as I'm taking on someone else's problems, then I add, "I'll be checking with you for updates. Daily at first, then, if things go well, weekly."

"Great," she says, and the look I get seems to invite me to make those reports face to face, which is fine with me.

"So, you'll move in the house, so you can parent these kids?" I ask. "I'm sure this joint has plenty of room."

"Tomorrow."

Then I turn to Prather. "Wire the money to my account." I go into my phone and retrieve the account and routing numbers and write them down for him, then continue. "You've got enough cash in the house to pay Hank the sixty grand plus interest you owe him. Just make it an even sixty-six thousand...so get it out. Then you're going to pack and drive out of here and not come back until you get a clean bill of health from a doc, who'll I recommend by morning. Call Tatya by noon and get a name, understand? And, by the way, get rid of the hidden hard drive on your computer...you know, the one with all the porn. You're one of the world's best with computers, Prather, but my people are even better. They've mirrored that drive, so we have that to hold over your worthless head."

He's beginning to get it, and his tone is now begging. "I don't want to go to jail."

"What you don't want is for your business to be ruined, for your reputation to be ruined, and far more importantly for your children to be ruined worse than you've already done. Now get on the phone to your banker and get the money wired."

"It's after hours," he says, looking hopeful. "Besides, I only owe you two million four hundred fifty thousand…remember the advance?"

"Do it, and you're right about the amount…a deal's a deal, even though you don't seem to honor them. Get your banker on the phone…you know they'll do whatever you need done."

With resignation, he does so, and while he's doing so, I call Pax. "Hey, I need confirmation that two-point-four-fifty mil hits the bank in the Caymans. Can do?" I ask, and he confirms that he can.

"Congrats," he says, and hangs up.

"It's done," Prather says, and hangs up about the same time as I do.

"Now, let's go get you packed," I say.

"And don't fucking come back!" Portia screams at him.

"Gee whiz," Wedgeworth mumbles, "it's no wonder I'm so screwed up."

He rises and stumbles toward the door and I follow, chastising him as we go. "Don't even think there's any, and I mean *any*, excuse for you being such a worthless prick. I'm going with you and will watch you pack."

We climb another set of curved stairs, at least ten feet wide under a chandelier the size of a Volkswagen, from the entry to the second floor. I follow him down a long hallway, then reach out and stop him. "Which room is Athena's?"

He points to a door and I walk over and knock on it, and Tenee immediately answers.

"Did you kill him?" she asks, not knowing he's six feet from me.

Chapter Thirty Six

"Tenee!" Wedgeworth manages, sounding shocked, as he should be, and she looks over.

"I want you dead," she shouts.

I lay a hand on her shoulder. "He's moving out, and you'll not see him for a long time, and maybe never again unless he gets well and lots of doctors say he is. Your mother is going to a hospital to get some help for her drinking. Tatya will be staying with you kids. And I'll be checking on you and your brother and sister."

She falls into my chest, hugs me, and begins to sob.

"It's gonna be fine, Tenee. It will take some time, but Tatya is a good woman and she'll watch over you, and you'll mind her, right?"

She nods her head.

"I mean that too. You've got to mind her and you've got to be a good kid. I'll be checking on that too."

"I will, I promise."

I gently shove her back inside her room and pull the door shut.

"Pack," I snap at Wedgeworth.

"Gee whiz," I hear him mumble, as he heads for the master bedroom.

While he's packing I ask him who, at CalGeoCyber, he wants to take over the company in his absence, and he says it has to be the chief counsel, Blumenthal. So I inform him I'll be meeting with Norval Blumenthal, who will be instructed to draw up an agreement for Tatya, to handle the request to the judge for the order for her temporary custody of the kids, and to contact Wedgeworth, him, to confirm his temporary appointment as CEO. I assure him that I'll only tell Blumenthal that it's all health related, which is true, as insanity is a health issue.

Skip and I follow Wedgeworth to see that he checks into the Biltmore hotel. He does, and what a surprise, he seems both eager and anxious to part company.

It's after ten when we rejoin our buddies at Lucky's, but not too late for me to order a rare New York steak, a baked, and grilled spinach, which I chase down with a local Firestone beer, while Skip manages to destroy a like steak, a lobster, and an exotic pot pie of some kind.

I hand a paper sack over to Hank. "Here's the dough Wedgeworth owes you, plus interest. You're buying supper."

"Wow," he manages, peeking inside the sack and smiling as if he just hit the lottery. "You bet your sweet ass I'm buying."

We decide to split up as I don't trust Wedgeworth not to be stupid enough to try and have his bodyguards, or some independent contractor, resolve his problem by sending us all five to Valhalla. Skip and I head into town and find a hotel and separate rooms on separate floors, while Madman, Wetback and Hank go out to Goleta and split up in two motels. The plan is to drive to Vegas in the morning, presuming the money's in the Caymen bank.

Knowing Pax is an early riser, I call first thing, and as promised, the dough is there. I owe an even million to my four buddies. I'll pay Pax a quarter mil for his trouble, which leaves a million two for the brains of the outfit…but since the outfit has little brains, I'll keep it.

I spend a half hour with Blumenthal and leave him a little perplexed to say the least, but he finally calls Wedgeworth at the Biltmore and looks even more bamboozled as Prather confirms all. My final words to Blumenthal are, "Mr. Wedgeworth has a plethora of personal problems that he and his wife have to work out, which is the reason for the custody agreement. For your ears only, some of those problems can ruin this company and if I were forced to divulge them, everyone here would be out of a job and the company's stock would be worthless. Do you understand?"

He eyes me carefully, and with great suspicion, but nods his head.

So I continue, "I'll be checking with Tatya, and you, to see that everything remains as Prather and I have agreed." When your talking to attorneys you can use words like plethora.

"You're blackmailing him," Blumenthal accuses.

"Into doing exactly the right thing? That doesn't sound like blackmail to me." I laugh, but he's not amused.

He lowers his head and glowers at me over his glasses. "I don't know what's going on, but I plan to find out. This is very, very irregular."

"I'm sure the CEO makes more than the Chief Counsel, so if I were you I wouldn't look the proverbial gift horse in the mouth."

I excuse myself, with Blumenthal not knowing whether to thank me or call the cops.

All that's a step in the right direction.

But the payouts are not over.

Toby Bartlett was an innocent in the missing airplane fiasco, paid the ultimate price in a horrible way, and left a young mother to raise two kids. I'll deliver a quarter mil cash to her as well, as Toby was a player in the scenario, albeit an unwilling one. I owe Carmen eight grand and will deposit an even ten in her American account, which is probably not enough as she took far more risk than she signed up to take. We were welcomed with open arms into a very deserving orphanage, Solange del Argentina Norte, and I'm dropping a check in the mail to those folks for another ten grand. So, what the hell, nine hundred thirty grand ain't bad, and I'll pay tax on that, which will knock it down to a hair over six hundred thou, spendable, for a month's work. I can live with that.

And hell, I didn't even get shot once.

The good news—not that six hundred thou spendable isn't good news—we learn when we wander into Pax's Vegas office. The repairman has been contacted by a wealthy investor who's headquartered in the big city of New York, and it seems his daughter has failed to return from the University of California at Berkeley, and he wants her found...as well as the seven million that's disappearing out of the trust fund her grandfather left her upon his demise.

Sounds like it might be worth a few bucks, and besides, I've only spent one weekend in New York.

Gee whiz, I'm going to the big city.

L. J. Martin is the acclaimed, award-winning, author of over 40 novels and non-fiction books. He was raised in the deserts of California and wrangled and packed horses throughout the Sierra, and later rode and hunted Montana, where he now lives with his wife, NYT bestselling romantic suspense and historical romance author Kat Martin. L. J. was in real estate development for much of his life, selling over one hundred million dollars in transactions the last year he worked in the field. He's traveled the world over, sailed his own ketch, been car wrecked, plane wrecked, beat, and bent…and dealt with some of the most powerful companies in the country. He knows the boardrooms and the backrooms of America, and her deep forests and wild high country. In wilder times he was the guest of many a *jusgados* but that's another story for another day. The Martins winter in California when not travelling for research on their novels.

More great action-adventure novels from acclaimed author L. J. Martin

(click on the title or the cover to go to a purchase link)

The Repairman (1st in the Repairman Series). No. 1 on Amazon's crime list! Got a problem? Need it fixed? Call Mike Reardon, the repairman, just don't ask him how he'll get it done. Trained as a Recon Marine to search and destroy, he brings those skills to the tough streets of America's cities. If you like your stories spiced with fists, guns, and beautiful women, this is the fast paced novel for you.

The Bakken (2nd in the Repairman Series). No. 1 on Amazon's crime list! The stand alone sequel to The Repairman. Mike Reardon gets a call from his old CO in Iraq, who's now a VP at an oil well service company in North America's hottest boomtown, and dope and prostitution is running wild and costing the company millions, and the cops are overwhelmed. If you have a problem, and want it fixed, call the repairman…just don't ask him what he's gonna do.

Quiet Ops. "…knows crime and how to write about it…you won't put this one down." Elmore Leonard
L. J. Martin with America's No. 1 bounty hunter, Bob Burton, brings action-adventure in double doses. From Malibu to West Palm Beach, Brad Benedick hooks 'em up and haul 'em in…in chains.

Crimson Hit. Dev Shannon loves his job, travels, makes good money, meets interesting people…then hauls them in cuffs and chains to justice. Only this time it's personal.

Bullet Blues. Shannon normally doesn't work in his hometown, but this time it's a friend who's gone missing, and he's got to help…if he can stay alive long enough. Tracking down a stolen yacht, which takes him all the way to Jamaica, he finds himself deep in the dirty underbelly of the drug trade.

Windfall. From the boardroom to the bedroom, David Drake has fought his way…nearly…to the top. From the jungles of Vietnam, to the vineyards of Napa, to the grit and grime of the California oil fields, he's clawed his way up. The only thing missing is the woman he's loved most of his life. Now, he's going to risk it all to win it all, or end up on the very bottom where he started. This business adventure-thriller will leave you breathless.

Bloodlines. When an ancient document is found deep under the streets of Manhattan, no one can anticipate the wild results. A businessman is forced to search deep into his past and reach back to those who once were wronged, and redeem for them what is right and just. There's a woman he's yearned for, and must have, but all is against them...and someone want him dead.

The Clint Ryan Series:

El Lazo. John Clinton Ryan, young, fresh to the sea from Mystic, Conetticut, is shipwrecked on the California coast...and blamed for the catastrophe. Hunted by the hide, horn and tallow captains, he escapes into the world of the vaquero, and soon gains the name El Lazo, for his skill with the lasso. A classic western tale of action and adventure, and the start of the John Clinton Ryan, the Clint Ryan series.

Against the 7th Flag. Clint Ryan, now skilled with horse and reata, finds himself caught up in the war of California revolution, Manifest Destiny is on the march, and he's in the middle of the fray, with friends on one side and countrymen on the other...it's fight or be killed, but for whom?

The Devil's Bounty. On a trip to buy horses for his new ranch in the wilds of swampy Central California, Clint finds himself compelled to help a rich Californio don who's beautiful daughter has been kidnapped and hauled to the barracoons of the Barbary Coast. Thrown in among the Chinese tongs, Australian Sidney Ducks, and the dredges of the gold rush failures, he soon finds an ally in a slave, now a newly freedman, and it's gunsmoke and flashing blades to fight his way to free the senorita.

The Benicia Belle. Clint signs on as master-at-arms on a paddle wheeler plying the Sacramento from San Francisco to the gold fields. He's soon blackmailed by the boats owner and drawn to a woman as dangerous and beautiful as the sea he left behind. Framed for a crime he didn't commit, he has only one chance to exact a measure of justice and…revenge.

Shadow of the Grizzly. "Martin has produced a landlocked, Old West version of Peter Benchley's *Jaws*," Publisher's Weekly. When the Stokes brothers, the worst kind of meat hunters, stumble on Clint's horse ranch, they are looking to take what he has. A wounded griz is only trying to stay alive, but he's a horrible danger to man and beast. And it's Clint, and his crew, including a young boy, who face hell together.

Condor Canyon. On his way to Los Angeles, a pueblo of only one thousand, Clint is ambushed by a posse after the abductor of a young woman. Soon he finds himself trading his Colt and his skill for the horses he seeks…now if he can only stay alive to claim them.

The Montana Series – The Clan:

Stranahan. "A good solid fish-slinging gunslinging read," William W. Johnstone. Sam Stranahan's an honest man who finds himself on the wrong side of the law, and the law has their own version of right and wrong. He's on his way to find his brother, and walks into an explosive case of murder. He has to make sure justice is done...with or without the law.

McCreed's Law. Gone...a shipment of gold and a handful of passengers from the Transcontinental Railroad. Found...a man who knows the owlhoots and the Indians who are holding the passengers for ransom. When you want to catch outlaws, hire an outlaw...and get the hell out of the way.

Wolf Mountain. The McQuades are running cattle, while running from the tribes who are fresh from killing Custer, and they know no fear. They have a rare opportunity, to get a herd to Mile's and his troops at the mouth of the Tongue...or to die trying. And a beautiful woman and her father, of questionable background, who wander into camp look like a blessing, but trouble is close on their trail...as if the McQuades don't have trouble enough.

O'Rourke's Revenge. Surviving the notorious Yuma Prison should be enough trouble for any man...but Ryan O'Rourke is not just any man. He wants blood, the blood of those who framed him for a crime he didn't commit. He plans to extract revenge, if it costs him all he has left, which is less than nothing...except his very life.

McKeag's Mountain. Old Bertoldus Prager has long wanted McKeag's Mountain, the Lucky Seven Ranch his father had built, and seven hired guns tried to take it the hard way, leaving Dan McKeag for dead...but he's a McKeag, and clings to life. They should have made sure...for now it will cost them all, or he'll die trying, and Prager's in his sights as well.

The Nemesis Series:

Nemesis. The fools killed his family...then made him a lawman! There are times when it pays not to be known, for if they had, they'd have killed him on the spot. He hadn't seen his sister since before the war, and never met her husband and two young daughters...but when he heard they'd been murdered, it was time to come down out of the high country and scatter the country with blood and guts.

Mr. Pettigrew. Beau Boone, starving, half a left leg, at the end of his rope, falls off the train in the hell-on-wheels town of Nemesis. But Mr. Pettigrew intervenes. Beau owes him, but does he owe him his very life? Can a one-legged man sit shotgun in one of the toughest saloons on the Transcontinental. He can, if he doesn't have anything to lose.

The Ned Cody Series:

Buckshot. Young Ned Cody takes the job as City Marshal...after all, he's from a long line of lawmen. But they didn't face a corrupt sheriff and his half-dozen hard deputies, a half-Mexican half-Indian killer, and a town who thinks he could never do the job.

Mojave Showdown. Ned Cody goes far out of his jurisdiction when one of his deputies is hauled into the hell's fire of the Mojave Desert by a tattooed Indian who could track a deer fly and live on his leavings. He's the toughest of the tough, and the Mojave has produced the worst. It's ride into the jaws of hell, and don't worry about coming back.

Made in the USA
Charleston, SC
29 May 2014